The Silver Locket

Also by Tom Milton

Orphans of War

Invisible Wounds

Leave of Absence

Outside the Gate

The Golden Door

Sara's Laughter

A Shower of Roses

Infamy

All the Flowers

The Admiral's Daughter

No Way to Peace

The Silver Locket

Tom Milton

NEPPERHAN PRESS, LLC
YONKERS, NY

Published by Nepperhan Press, LLC
P.O. Box 1448, Yonkers, NY 10702
nepperhan@optonline.net
nepperhan.com

PUBLISHER'S NOTE
This is a work of fiction. Names, characters, places, and incidents are the product of the author's imagination or are used fictitiously, and any resemblance to actual persons, living or dead, events, or locales is entirely coincidental.

Printed in the United States of America

Library of Congress Control Number: 2016912445

ISBN 978-0-9899571-7-5

Cover art was licensed from Publitek, Inc.

For Marie

God forgives everyone, he offers new possibilities to everyone, he showers his mercy on everyone who asks for it. We are the ones who do not know how to forgive.

Pope Francis, *The Name of God is Mercy*

Yonkers, 2016

ONE

As SHE WALKED along the path that overlooked the river, within the sanctuary of a college campus, Esperanza felt safe, which she wouldn't have felt on the streets of her neighborhood. There she would have kept her guard up, but here she relaxed and enjoyed the beauty of the sunset over the Palisades. She paused for a moment to admire the way the crimson light traversed the water, and after murmuring a prayer of thanks for being admitted to the college, she continued walking along the path, intending to go a little farther before she turned around.

Then, suddenly, a strong arm locked around her neck and cut off her air. She struggled but the hand of another arm grabbed one of her wrists and brutally twisted her arm while the lock around her neck tightened until she lost consciousness.

When she came to she was lying on her back with something wrapped around her eyes to blindfold her and something wadded in her mouth to gag her. She realized that she was naked, and she tried to resist, but someone heavy was pinning her arms down with his knees and clamping her wrists down with his hands. She tried to kick, but both of her legs were being held and spread. In her desperate state, she prayed to Our Lady of Guadalupe to rescue her, but that didn't help. She felt the hard bare knees of someone against her thighs, and then a hard object that was much too big for her was violently forced into her, tearing her flesh and impaling her. Transfixed, she choked on her stifled cries, and she prayed for mercy. But the guy banged her as if he was trying to drive a stake all the way through her.

He finally stopped with a shudder and a groan, and for a while he just lay on her, a dead weight. But then another guy said: "You had your turn. It's my turn now." By the direction of his voice,

Esperanza guessed he was holding her right leg, and while the first guy traded places with him, she had a chance to kick at them. But then her leg was held again, and the other guy got on top of her. It took him only a moment to ram into her and start banging her as if he was trying to outperform the first guy. It took him less time before he stopped with a shudder and a groan, and at that point Esperanza prayed that they were done.

But then the guy who was holding her left leg had his turn. The only thing different was that he bit her nipples roughly before he rammed into her. He also made more noise than they did, and one of them told him to keep it down. By then she guessed there were four of them, and the guy who was pinning her arms would be next. She summoned the courage to bear the ordeal, but she was cowed by the possibility that once they had all taken a turn they would start over with the first guy, and it would never end.

The third guy finally got off her, and she braced herself for what she hoped was the last guy.

"Come on, it's your turn," one of them told him.

"I don't want to," the guy who was pinning her arms said.

"What's the matter? You can't get it up?"

"I just don't want to."

"Well, that's your choice," the guy who was evidently the leader said. "Do you guys want another turn?"

"No, I'm wiped out."

"I am too. Let's get out of here."

"Okay," the leader said. "But I'm going to do something before we leave her."

She was afraid he was going to kill her, but at the same time she wished he would. She couldn't imagine living after this.

A few moments later she felt a stream of warm water falling onto her naked belly.

The other two guys who had taken their turns laughed raucously. The guy who was pinning her arms said: "You shouldn't do that."

"I shouldn't? Who says?" The water kept falling.

"She deserves it," one of the other guys said.

"Yeah, she asked for it," another one said.

"She's a hot little spic," the leader said with authority. "So I have to cool her off."

"She was a virgin," the guy who was pinning her arms said.

"Naw, she wasn't. She's a *puta*, as they say in their language."

"Then why was there blood?"

"Who the hell knows? She might be starting her period."

"Come on, let's go," one of them said.

"Before we go," the leader said, "we need to tie her hands, so we have time to get away."

"She's not going to come after us."

"No, but she could take off the blindfold and see enough to identify us."

"What can we use to tie her hands?"

"Her bra," the leader said.

She lay there still while they tied her hands. Whoever did it bound her very tight. And then they finally left her.

For a long time she didn't move. She only wanted to find a spot along the path where she could throw herself off the cliff and onto the railroad tracks below. She finally sat up and started working on the knots of her bra.

When her hands were free she pulled the wad out of her mouth and unwrapped her eyes. They had used her panties to gag her and her shirt to blindfold her.

Her chest and her belly were wet with urine, but she didn't have anything to wipe it off. They had folded her jeans and put them under her buttocks, propping her up. The jeans had blood on them. If she put on these clothes and returned to the heart of the campus, people would wonder what had happened to her. That was bad enough, but the thought of going home in her soiled clothes made her cringe with fear. If she couldn't clean herself up before going home, she might as well throw herself off the cliff.

As she sat there she instinctively reached for the locket that she wore on a chain around her neck. It was a silver locket with a picture of Our Lady of Guadalupe inside, a gift from her parents for her *quinceañera*. But it wasn't there. By now it was dark, and the locket could have been on the ground beside her, but she didn't see it. She crawled around, combing her fingers through the grass, praying that she would find it, but she didn't find it. She wondered if one of those guys had taken it, though that wasn't likely. If the locket was found in their possession, it could be used as evidence against them.

After a while she resolved to come back first thing in the morning and look for the locket. It had to be somewhere in the area.

She was still naked, but she wasn't in a hurry to put on her clothes since no one could see her from the path. They had taken her into a hollow that was screened from the path by huge boulders, with trees on the other three sides. So they had no risk of being seen by anyone. It made her wonder if they had been waiting for a lone girl to come along.

From the turmoil of her raw emotions, her top priority emerged: she had to hide what had happened to her. No one, not even a priest, could know about it.

Finally an idea came to her. She had started college only a month ago, but there was a girl she had met in freshman seminar and gotten friendly with. Her name was Griselda, and her family lived up the river in Haverstraw, which was too far away for her to commute, so she was in the dormitory. If she was in her room now, Esperanza could go there and take a shower and wash her clothes. She only had to make up a story to explain why there was blood on her jeans and why she smelled like urine.

She pulled on her panties, which were damp with her saliva, and she hooked her bra behind her back, wincing at the pain of her twisted arm. She put on her shirt, though her torso was still damp with urine. The hardest part was getting into the bloody jeans. She found her shoes and looked around for her backpack. It was on the ground, not far from the spot where they had pinned her, and her phone was in a pocket of the backpack.

Checking her watch, she saw that it was quarter of eight, an hour after her mother would expect her to be home. She didn't know what to tell her mother, so first she texted Griselda asking if she was in her room now. Within five minutes Griselda responded that she was. With further messages they arranged for Esperanza to meet Griselda in her room.

Then she texted her mother saying she wouldn't be home for an hour or so. At least that way her mother wouldn't be worrying about her.

By walking across the lawns of the campus she avoided meeting people on the sidewalks, and she reached the security desk of the women's dormitory without encountering anyone. The woman at the desk hardly looked at her as she phoned Griselda for permission to admit a visitor.

Climbing the stairs, she turned her face away from a girl she met coming down. She didn't know the girl, but whoever it was, she didn't want to make eye contact with her.

Griselda had a single room, which she hadn't requested but was given because they ran out of double rooms while there were still unoccupied singles. And they charged her only the rate she would have paid for sharing a double.

The door opened as soon as she knocked on it, and there was Griselda, whose big brown eyes got even bigger at the sight of Esperanza.

"*Madre de Dios! Qué te pasó?*" Griselda cried with a look of concern.

"I had an accident," Esperanza said, entering the room. "I wasn't expecting my period, so I wasn't prepared."

"*Entiendo.* I've had that kind of accident." Griselda frowned, wrinkling her nose. "But you smell like pee."

"I was so upset, I peed in my pants."

Griselda nodded sympathetically. "I sometimes do that when I laugh too hard."

"I wasn't laughing."

"Actually, you look like you were crying."

"I *was* crying. I can't get on the bus in these clothes."

"Well, if I didn't know you, I wouldn't want to sit next to you."

They were speaking in Spanish but with very different accents. Griselda spoke rapidly, with short vowels and truncated words, whereas Esperanza spoke slowly, with long vowels and complete words. They often joked with each other about the differences between the ways Dominicans and Mexicans spoke the language, but they had no trouble understanding each other. In fact, they preferred speaking in Spanish.

They moved a little away from the door, still standing since out of respect for the furniture Esperanza wasn't going to sit down.

"I need to take a shower and wash these clothes," she told her friend.

"*Claro.* You can't go home like this." Griselda paused, looking as if she had some doubts. "But aren't you usually home by now?"

"I am, except on Wednesdays, when I have a class that ends at five forty."

"It's almost eight now. Where did you go after class?"

"I went for a walk along the path that overlooks the river."

"I like that walk. Believe it or not, I sometimes go for a walk there early in the morning. You can't see the sunrise, but you can see it reflected off the Palisades."

"I have that view from my bedroom at home. I mean, if I get up early enough."

"So is that where you had the accident?"

"Yeah." It was true, and not lying about where it had happened made her feel a little less bad for lying about what had happened.

"Well, let's get you into the shower," Griselda said. "You can wear my robe. And while you're showering, I'll put your clothes into the machine."

"I don't want to get your robe dirty."

"*No te preocupes.* Even though this is a women's dorm, you can't walk down the hall naked."

Before, she might have joked about what might happen if she walked down the hall of the dorm naked, but not now. She only said: "Okay."

She undressed in front of Griselda, believing there was nothing her friend could see that would contradict the story she had told her. The blood was still sticky, but the urine was dry and what those guys had discharged into her no longer leaked out.

She put on the robe and after accepting a tampon she followed Griselda down the hall to the communal bathroom, hoping no one else would be there. By nature, she was a private person, and now she needed more than ever not to be an object of public scrutiny.

Luckily, she had the bathroom all to herself, and as she stood in the shower with the hot water flowing from her head to her toes, she felt at least superficially cleansed from what had happened to her. But deep within her she felt degraded and violated, and even worse, remembering how they had said she deserved it, she felt as if it had been her fault, though by the farthest stretch of her imagination she couldn't see how it had been her fault. As much as she tried to convince herself that she was the innocent victim of a savage attack, she felt culpable, she felt as if she had committed a mortal sin.

She finally got out of the shower and dried herself. She had put the tampon in the pocket of the robe, and now she didn't know what to do with it. Maybe after being raped you were supposed to use a tampon, but the idea of sticking anything into her made her grimace. Yet if she didn't use the tampon, Griselda might wonder about her story. So she dropped it into the trash.

She trudged down the hall to Griselda's room. Since the door was partly open, she walked in and found Griselda sitting at her desk with a textbook in front of her.

"You look better," Griselda said brightly.

"I feel better," she lied.

"Your clothes should be ready in about ten minutes, and then I can put them into the drier."

"Just tell me where to go and I'll put them into the drier."

"No, I'll do it. You should lie down."

"I'm only having my period."

"I know, but—" Griselda stopped as if she didn't want to say what she was thinking.

"What?" Esperanza said, wanting to head off any speculation.

"I just have a feeling it's something worse than a period."

"It's not. I had an accident, and you know what it's like to have an accident."

"Yeah, I do. It's embarrassing."

"Well, thanks for the tampon," Esperanza said, reinforcing her story about the accident.

"*De nada*," Griselda said.

They listened to music for a while, and then Griselda went to put the clothes into the drier. Esperanza finally lay down and closed her eyes, wishing she could turn the clock back to the time when a happy girl was walking along the path that overlooked the river, admiring the sunset. But she knew she would never be that girl again. In fact, if she happened to meet that girl, she wouldn't even recognize her.

There was a bus stop outside the entrance of the college, and Esperanza waited there for a bus that would take her to downtown Yonkers. She waited only about five minutes, and as soon as she was on the bus she texted her mother, saying she was on her way home. Her mother acknowledged receipt of the message, saying: "*Bien, gracias.*"

As she rode down the hill she concocted a story to explain to her mother why she was late, drawing on material that neither of her parents were familiar with and therefore were unlikely to question. She had virtually never lied to them, and just the thought of lying to them made her feel even worse about what had happened to her, compounding her shame and intensifying her despair. But imagining how her parents would react if she told the truth made her feel it was necessary to lie, if only to preserve what little remained of her human dignity.

She got off at the stop after St. Joseph's Hospital, where her mother worked as a nursing assistant. Her mother always had the shift from eight to four, which during the week allowed her to make breakfast for her children in the morning and to prepare dinner for them in the evening. Her father wouldn't be home now since he worked as the sous-chef in a highly rated Italian restaurant on Main Street, where he had started as a kitchen helper. He usually didn't get home until almost midnight and he slept late, so there were days when Esperanza didn't see him. She hoped that at least for a day or two she wouldn't see him.

Her family lived in an apartment building on South Broadway that had been renovated only a few years ago. Before her father's promotion to sous-chef, they had lived in a building farther south, with only two bedrooms, and they had been cramped, but now with three bedrooms they had enough space, and the rent was still very reasonable.

Esperanza let herself into the building and climbed the stairs to the third floor, hearing the sounds of mariachi music from an apartment on the second floor. The music was happy, in contrast to the lives of most people in Mexico, as she perceived them. Her father, who had emigrated from there at the age of eighteen, was lucky enough to be sponsored by his older brother, who had established a successful landscaping business in New Rochelle. Esperanza and her younger brother Charro were born in Yonkers, so they were automatically U.S. citizens. Their parents, after years of study and legal process, finally became U.S. citizens. So now they could travel to Mexico and visit the city of Puebla, where they were both from. But so far, due to the complexity of work schedules and school schedules, they hadn't finalized any plans for such a trip.

Her mother must have recognized her steps in the hall since she was on the other side of the door to greet her, wearing an apron that was streaked with corn flour. She was a stout woman, a few inches shorter than Esperanza, and she gave the impression that she would be hard to push around.

"*Por qué llegas tan tarde?*" her mother asked her after showing a flicker of relief that she was safely home.

"I had to meet with my advisor," she lied.

"Your advisor works so late?"

"Yeah. They work until seven."

"It's after nine now."

"I then had to meet with a financial aid counselor. They work until eight," she added.

"Well, you should have told me in advance."

"I didn't know how long it would take."

Her mother examined her closely with unblinking eyes, but she didn't know enough of the college's processes to question her story. "Have you had dinner?"

"No. But I'm not hungry." She realized immediately that it was a mistake to say she wasn't hungry, which would make her mother wonder if there was something wrong with her.

"Are you all right?" Again, her mother examined her closely.

"Yeah, I'm just not hungry. I had a big lunch."

"What did you eat?"

"A burger and fries."

Her mother shook her head as if she disapproved of such food. Her mother, with knowledge from her training, often talked about how American junk food had caused the epidemic of obesity in Mexico. "Well, you can at least help me clean up."

She followed her mother into the kitchen and helped her clean up. While drying a dish, she realized that without her there for dinner her mother had the company only of Charro, who wasn't allowed to use his smartphone at mealtimes and therefore wolfed down his food so that he could return to his room and escape into the unreal world of the internet. He was a sophomore at Yonkers High School, and he did well in math but not so well in other subjects. Except for his being a techie nerd, Esperanza had no major problem with him.

For a while she stayed with her mother in the living room to keep her company. Her mother liked to watch the telenovelas from Mexico, so on one of the Spanish language channels they watched a telenovela that her mother had been following. Years ago, Esperanza had tried to get her mother to watch American soap operas to improve her English, but her mother argued that she had to speak English all day at work and in the evening she wanted to relax. She had also tried speaking English with her mother, but that hadn't worked. Though Esperanza was fluent in English, she felt more comfortable speaking Spanish with her mother. She spoke English with her brother, except when he was annoying her.

When the telenovela episode was over, she rose from the sofa and announced that she was going to bed—another mistake, since she usually didn't go to bed so early.

"Are you all right?" her mother asked her again with a frown of concern.

"Yeah, I'm fine. I'm just a little more tired than usual. Maybe from talking with my advisor and the financial aid counselor," she added to reinforce her story.

"Well, if you're tired, you should go to bed."

She leaned over and kissed her mother goodnight, and then she went down the hall to her room, passing the room of her brother, from which she could hear the inhuman sounds of whatever electronic game he was playing.

In her room she changed into the long tee shirt that she used as a nightgown, and she got into bed and turned off the light. She pulled the covers over her and curled up into a ball of anguish. Wanting never to wake up again, she prayed for a merciful death in her sleep.

But she had trouble going to sleep. She kept remembering how they had banged her as if they were trying to drive a stake all the way through her.

She was still awake when her father came home. She heard the sounds of her parents talking in the living room, but she couldn't understand what they were saying. They always talked for a while after her father got home, and then together they went to bed.

Eventually, she went to sleep, but she was awakened by a nightmare in which those guys were nailing her hands and feet down, with her legs spread, so they wouldn't have to expend energy to hold her down. And then the first guy loomed above her, holding a sledgehammer in one hand and a long spike in the other hand.

She awoke with a scream, which must have been loud enough to wake her mother, who opened the door and came into the room and asked: "*Qué te pasó?*"

"I had a nightmare."

"What about?"

"Oh, it was nothing. I mean, it was stupid."

Her mother waited for details.

"Some guys were threatening to push me off a cliff."

"Were they guys you know?"

"I didn't scc their faces."

"Well, it sounds like a typical nightmare." Her mother lay a comforting hand on her forehead and said: *"Ahora vuelves a dormir."*

And she finally did go back to sleep.

When she woke up the next morning she hoped that the whole experience had been a nightmare, but the pain in her vagina confirmed that it had been real: four guys had attacked her, and three of them had raped her. That was the reality, and now she had to deal with it.

After counting the days since her last period she realized with a stab of fear that they could have made her pregnant. They had shot three rounds of semen into her, and there was a high probability that one of those millions of spermatozoa had found an egg. And if she was pregnant, she would have no way of hiding what had happened to her. All she could do was wait about two weeks and take a pregnancy test, and if it was positive, she would have to kill herself in a way that prevented anyone from finding out that she was pregnant.

"*Nuestra Señora,*" she prayed, "*no quiero ser embarazada.*"

She finally got up and faced the day. She had a class at ten fifteen but before then she had to go and search for her locket. She believed that if she found the locket it would be a sign that her prayer would be granted.

It was almost seven thirty, and her mother was still in the kitchen, making sure that her children had breakfast. Charro was there, eating a tortilla wrap and spilling the contents onto his plate. In front of him was a cup of hot chocolate, which their mother made for them every morning. Elsewhere on the table were a plate of tortillas, a bowl of beans, a container of yogurt, and a bowl of orange wedges.

"*Dormiste bien?*" her mother asked.

"Oh, yeah. I didn't have another nightmare."

"Well, I have to go to work now. If you're going to be late tonight, please let me know in advance."

"I won't be late tonight. My last class ends at two thirty."

Her mother went to change into her scrubs, and then she returned to say goodbye. In her absence Charro had taken out his smartphone and was fully engrossed in a stupid game. Ignoring his minor violation of the house rules, her mother kissed him and Esperanza, telling them both to have a good day.

When her mother had left, Esperanza took a tortilla and ate it plain. She ate a few orange wedges, and then she got up from the table, saying: "I'm going to the college."

Her brother actually responded, asking: "Why so early?"

"I have to meet with a professor. You can leave the food on the table for *papá*."

She went to the bathroom, and then she went into her room and loaded her backpack with the notebooks she would need that day. At first she had taken textbooks to class, but after learning that her professors didn't use them in the classroom she left them at home, which made her backpack a lot lighter.

She caught the next bus across the street from where she had gotten off yesterday, and she rode to the college along with students who must have had classes at eight thirty. When she got off the bus and entered the campus, it was different: it was no longer a sanctuary, and it no longer promised what it had before yesterday.

She followed the sidewalk around Morrissey Hall and crossed the parking lot and the soccer field to get to the path. She paused to look across the river at the Palisades, which were lit up by the low sun, but they were no longer magnificent. They were only walls of crumbling rock.

When she got to where the guy had grabbed her, she stopped

and caught her breath to avoid fainting. It was as if the guy still had his arm locked around her neck.

Cautiously, she found her way to the hollow. She stopped at the spot where they had pinned her. It was easy to identify since the grass was flattened, and there were scuff marks around it. She imagined herself lying there, gagged and blindfolded, completely helpless. And she began to cry, believing that her life would now be filled only with sorrow.

She appealed to Our Lady, asking: "Why did you let them do that to me?"

She waited, but there was no response.

On her hands and knees she began searching for the locket. She started at the spot where they had raped her, and then she moved methodically in concentric circles around the spot, determined to cover every inch of the area. She didn't keep track of the time, not caring if she missed her class. The only thing that mattered was finding the locket.

It was almost noon when she finally stopped. She had searched the area, inch by inch, repeatedly. She had even gone into a wooded area that was more than thirty feet away from the spot on the chance that one of the guys, in a gesture of wanton cruelty, had flung the locket there. But she didn't find it there, and she didn't find it anywhere.

Giving up the search, she bowed her head to the ground and submitted to the loss of help from above. The locket had been taken away because she wasn't worthy of it. She deserved what had happened to her. And she was probably pregnant.

TWO

JEFFREY FELT LUCKY to be invited to join his teammates that afternoon in a round of clandestine beer drinking. Brandon and Scott were sophomores, while he and Kenny were only freshmen, but Kenny, his roommate, was a lot more outgoing than he was, so Kenny was already doing things with the older guys outside of practice. As members of the college's lacrosse team, they practiced every weekday in the fall to prepare for the spring season. They met on the field around two and left around five, depending on the coach's mood. And that afternoon they were out of the showers shortly after five.

Jeffrey was from Poughkeepsie, where his father owned a successful restaurant that catered to families, business people, and parents visiting their children at Vassar College. His mother helped him with the business, mainly with bookkeeping and financial matters. They were both natives of Poughkeepsie and were highly regarded members of their community. They attended the ten o'clock mass at Holy Trinity every Sunday, and they served as extraordinary ministers at least once a month. Their children went to church with them from the time when they were babies, and Jeffrey served as an altar boy until he started high school. Except to his parents, he never admitted that he liked it.

He was the youngest, with two older sisters, whose needs and interests dominated the life of the household, so he grew up observing instead of participating, and he was characterized by his teachers as quiet, shy, and sensitive. Concerned about his passivity, his father encouraged him to play sports, and in high school he became a valuable member of the lacrosse team. He liked the sport, though he didn't love it the way he loved reading, and he appreciated the benefits he derived from it: the exercise, the friendships, and the joy of winning.

His grades were good, and his test scores were good enough to give him a choice of where to go to college. Since he understood that his parents wanted him to go to a Catholic college, he applied to Marist, St. Bonaventure, and St. Catherine, and he was accepted by all of them. He wanted to be away from home, but not too far away, so he eliminated St. Bonaventure, and he didn't want to be too close, so he eliminated Marist and decided on St. Catherine, which was about an hour away from home on the Amtrak. It also had the advantage of a lower tuition than the other two colleges.

He had been at college for a month now, and he was doing well. He liked his courses, except for one, and he got along with Kenny, though it was becoming clear that they had nothing in common other than lacrosse. Among other differences, Kenny regarded girls as sex objects, maybe because he didn't have sisters, and he was always making comments about parts of their anatomy. Jeffrey wasn't a prude, and he felt what he considered a natural attraction to girls, but he also had respect for them, maybe because he did have sisters. Kenny talked as if he had scored a hundred times, and Jeffrey just listened, not revealing that he hadn't ever gone all the way with a girl.

That afternoon, as the four of them crossed the parking lot, with Brandon carrying a cooler, he looked forward to a brief escape from the drudgery of practice and conditioning.

"I hope the coach doesn't see us," Kenny said.

"Don't worry," Scott said. "He left for the day. He has to drive home to Melville."

Jeffrey didn't know where Melville was, but since the other three guys seemed to know, he assumed that it was on Long Island, where they were all from. A lot of the guys who played lacrosse were from Long Island, which was evidently the right distance for them to be away from home: not too far away, and not too close.

"It must take him two hours to get home," Brandon said. "It's rush hour."

"It's always a bitch at rush hour," Scott said.

"When I go home, I go at midnight," Kenny said. "But even then there's a lot of traffic."

"I'd never voluntarily live on Long Island," Brandon said. He was a big, powerful guy, and he carried the cooler, which was filled with ice, water, and beer, as if it was a notebook.

"Where would you live?" Scott asked.

"I'd live in the city."

"You mean Manhattan?"

"I don't mean Brooklyn. That's Long Island."

"But how would you afford to live in Manhattan?"

"I'd get a job on Wall Street."

They were all business majors, and the new dean had installed a trading room in the building where the school was located. The dean and several of the faculty had worked on Wall Street, and they promoted it, telling students how much money they could make there.

"You know," Scott said, "whenever a professor tells me how much money I could make on Wall Street, I wonder why he isn't still there, making all that money."

"Maybe he lost his job in the crash," Kenny said.

"Or maybe he made so much money," Brandon said, "that he can afford to work here."

Jeffrey didn't comment. Being from upstate, he sometimes felt like a hick with these guys, who had been doing things in the city since they were kids.

They followed Brandon to a path that overlooked the river. Jeffrey had seen the view from the campus, but from the path, with nothing in the way, it was even more spectacular. Admiring it, he fell behind the other guys.

After a while Brandon led them off the path and down to a hollow, behind some huge boulders, where they could drink beer without being seen by anyone. Of course they were under the drinking age, but that didn't matter since they all had fake IDs, including Jeffrey. What mattered was that as athletes they were supposed to be in training, and drinking beer wasn't part of the program.

They settled on the grass, and Brandon opened the cooler. He took out cans of ice-cold beer one at a time and handed them around. There was a sound of cracking cans open, and then sighs of pleasure, with Kenny saying: "Man, that tastes good."

"We deserve a break today," Brandon said.

"We've worked hard," Scott agreed.

"He busts our asses," Kenny said, referring to the coach. "But I guess it's good for us."

"It's good for us," Brandon said. "But so is this."

They drank a round, talking about sports and cars and smartphones, and then they drank another round. They were chugging the beer, and Jeffrey had trouble keeping up with them, but somehow he did.

At one point Brandon and Scott talked about a girl they had smuggled to their room a few weeks ago. She had come with them willingly, and they had taken turns with her. They described in pornographic detail what they had done with her.

Jeffrey wasn't so naïve as not to know that guys did such things, but he was shocked to learn that his teammates did such things.

"That was a blast," Brandon said.

"Yeah, she was insatiable. We could have used two more guys."

"I wish you'd invited me to join you," Kenny said.

"We'll invite you next time," Brandon said.

Jeffrey was feeling a little tipsy when Scott got up and headed for the woods, saying: "I have to pee."

"I wonder why," Brandon said.

On his way back Scott said: "I spotted quarry."

"You did?" Brandon said. "Where?"

"She's up on the path."

"Is she alone?"

"Yeah, she's alone. Should we talk her into joining us?"

"No, we'll make her join us."

Jeffrey wasn't sure he understood what they were saying, so he only listened and watched while Brandon got up and positioned himself below the path, waiting for Scott, who had moved back toward the woods, to give him a signal.

When he got the signal Brandon climbed up to the path, and for a while he was hidden by the boulders. Then he came back down with a girl slung over his shoulder like a sack of mulch.

Unable to believe his eyes, Jeffrey watched as Kenny and Scott undressed the girl, gagged her with her panties, and blindfolded her with her shirt while Brandon made a video of them, using his smartphone. Whatever he had done to her up on the path, the girl was unconscious.

"When she comes to," Brandon said, with his phone ready for the next scene, "we'll have to hold her down."

Aghast, Jeffrey stood there, still holding a can of beer.

"Come on," Brandon told him. "Your job is to pin her arms and hold her wrists."

At that point he could have made a run for it. But he knew that if he did, they would never again invite him to join them. In fact, they would make life so hard for him that he would have to quit lacrosse and maybe even drop out of college. And at that moment his fear of exclusion was stronger than his revulsion at what they were doing.

Like a robot he went over and did what Brandon ordered him to do. He positioned his knees on the girl's soft outstretched arms and clamped his hands onto her wrists just in time to prevent her from moving them.

When Brandon dropped his pants and clambered onto her, Jeffrey closed his eyes, but he couldn't close his ears to avoid hearing her cries of pain.

"What am I doing?" he asked himself as if he didn't know.

He protested only when Brandon started peeing on her, but they ignored him. They thought it was funny to add this insult to injury.

When they had tied her hands Jeffrey got up and followed his teammates back along the path, wondering if there was a spot where he could jump off and kill himself. For what he had done to that poor girl, he knew he could never forgive himself.

He stayed in their room while Kenny went out with the other guys to have dinner. Alone, he lay on his bed and imagined what his parents would think, and what his sisters would think, if they knew what he had done. He realized that he should have chosen his family over his teammates. But now, whether his family ever found out about it, he was excluded from them. He was completely isolated from all humanity.

He said he was sorry to the girl, but she wasn't there. He said it to his parents and his sisters, but they weren't there. He said it to God, but he couldn't believe that even with his infinite mercy God would forgive him. Again, he felt like killing himself, but that would only compound his sin, and he would be damned to eternity. He thought of devoting himself to the poor, but he didn't see how a lifetime of sacrifice could ever make up for what he had done.

He was still lying there in agony when Kenny returned. They had evidently gone in Brandon's car to a downtown pub, and Kenny was boisterously drunk.

"Hey, man," he said. "How did you like what we did to that little spic?"

Jeffrey said nothing, and turned away from him.

"Did you see how we nailed her?"

"No, I didn't. My eyes were closed."

"That's too bad. But you can see us in action. We made a video of the whole thing."

"You shouldn't have made a video of it." He remembered them making a video, but until now he hadn't thought about the video as evidence of what they had done. And he imagined what his parents and sisters would think if they saw a video of him pinning the arms of a girl being raped.

"Don't worry," Kenny said. "It doesn't show our faces. It only shows our equipment."

"What about the girl? Does it show her face?"

"Oh, yeah. And she looks like she was enjoying it."

"Enjoying it? She was crying in pain."

"That wasn't pain. It was pleasure. You don't know much about girls, do you," Kenny added.

Resisting the urge to tell his roommate that he knew a lot about girls from having grown up with two sisters, Jeffrey asked: "What are you going to do with the video?"

"We're going to post it on a website."

"You mean on Facebook?"

"They don't allow that kind of thing on Facebook. But there are sites that do allow it. In fact, there are sites that specialize in gang rapes."

"How do you know about them?"

"I watch videos on them," Kenny said as if it was a perfectly normal form of entertainment.

"Are you sure the video doesn't show our faces?"

"Yeah, I'm sure. You think we're dumb enough to post a video that shows our faces?"

"But it shows the girl's face."

"So?" By now Kenny was sitting on his bed.

"If people recognize her," Jeffrey said, "she'll be humiliated."

"Who the hell cares? She's just a spic."

Jeffrey didn't comment, but he wondered how he could have ever gotten along with this guy. He closed his eyes and tried to go to sleep. But he kept remembering how he had pinned the girl's arms while those guys raped her, and he felt as if he had pinned the arms of Jesus while they drove the nails into his hands.

The next morning he got up early and returned to the scene of the crime. He didn't know why, but maybe he needed to remind himself of what he had done. He stood at the spot where they had raped her, and he began to cry, not for himself but for the girl. He wished that somehow he could make her whole again.

As he looked around, something bright caught his eye from the edge of the woods, reflecting the sunlight. He walked over and bent down and picked it up. It was a silver locket on a broken silver chain, and he was sure it belonged to the girl.

He hesitated, wondering whether to leave it there or whether to take it. If he left it, then someone else might find it, and the girl would never recover it. But if he took it, he would be committed to returning it sooner or later. And when he returned it he would have to explain why he thought it was hers.

Imagining how the girl might feel if she never recovered the locket, he decided to take it, and he left the scene without looking to see what was inside it.

He went directly to the library, to a carrel in the back where he could have privacy. He sat in the chair and took out the locket and carefully opened it. Inside was a picture of the Blessed Mother in a rose robe and a blue mantle with gold stars. Assuming it was a particular rendering of the Blessed Mother, he did a search on the internet and found an image of Our Lady of Guadalupe that matched the picture inside the locket.

Its religious content confirmed his feeling that the locket was important to the girl and that she would be upset to lose it. He imagined her trying to explain to her mother, who had probably given it to her, how she had lost it.

More than ever, he felt committed to returning the locket to the girl, but he was nowhere near ready to confront her and admit to her that he was one of her assailants.

That afternoon, except when he had to work with them, he avoided Kenny, Brandon, and Scott. He didn't feel like practicing lacrosse, and he didn't make his usual effort. When practice was over, the coach asked him to stay for a minute. The coach was about his father's age, a tough man, who had played for one of the great teams at Syracuse.

"So what's the problem?" the coach asked him.

"What do you mean?" he asked as if he didn't understand.

"I mean the way you weren't here today."

"Oh, I have something on my mind."

"Can you tell me about it?"

"No, I can't," Jeffrey said.

"Then put it off your mind while you're out there practicing."

"Okay. I'll try."

"You won't try, you'll do it. Or you'll be off the team," the coach added. "Is that clear?"

He nodded. "Yeah."

As he plodded to the locker room he wished that the coach *would* kick him off the team so that he wouldn't have to deal with Brandon and Scott anymore. And he could request a change in roommates.

After taking a shower, instead of going back to his room, where he might encounter Kenny, he went outside the campus and walked south on Broadway, past St. John's Hospital and Untermeyer Park, and onto Roberts Avenue to Palisade Avenue, where there was a pizza place on the corner. He ordered a slice of pizza and a can of soda, which he carried to a booth. He sat there until the pizza was cool enough, and then he took a bite of it, forcing himself to eat it. He was relieved to be alone, but there was nothing to distract him from the memory of what he had done. It turned his stomach, and he ended up chucking the pizza into the garbage, where he wished he could follow it.

He was lying in bed when Kenny returned, and he pretended to be asleep to avoid talking with him. Kenny stayed up late, playing on his computer, maybe watching videos of gang rapes. It was impossible to tell.

The next morning, which was Friday, he had an eight-thirty class in the freshman seminar. As a matter of principle, most students avoided scheduling classes on Friday, but he had no choice since he had to keep his afternoons free for lacrosse practice. The course was being taught by Sister Maura, one of the few remaining nuns, and unlike the students she was always full of energy in the morning. Jeffrey liked her, and he trusted her, but he hadn't slept all night, and he had trouble paying attention. When she called on him with a question about the ethics of a situation he didn't have anything to say.

She asked him to stay after class, making him feel like he was back in elementary school. She waited until all the other students were gone, and then she asked: "Is something wrong?"

Responding as he had to the coach, he asked the professor: "What do you mean?"

"You weren't paying attention, and you weren't prepared."

"I didn't sleep much last night."

"Were you partying?"

"No. I just couldn't sleep."

She was a rugged woman with curly gray hair and acute gray eyes, and she gazed at him as if she could detect something. "You want to talk about it?"

"There's nothing to talk about," he said, avoiding her eyes.

"I have a feeling there is. And my feelings are usually right," she added.

Before he could stop himself he said: "Well, there *is* something, but I can't tell you about it."

"Why can't you?"

"You're not a priest."

"I'm not a priest. I'm a nun."

"So you can't give me absolution."

"I can't give you absolution, but maybe I can help you."

"What if I told you and you couldn't help me?"

"You wouldn't lose anything."

"I could lose you as a teacher. I mean, if you knew what I did, you wouldn't want me as a student."

She looked at him for a long time without saying anything, and then she said: "So you did something really bad?"

"It was worse than really bad. It was unforgivable."

"Are you a Catholic?"

"I was raised as a Catholic."

"Then you should know that nothing you could ever do is unforgivable."

"Well, maybe God can forgive me, but I can't forgive myself."

"You mean you're holding yourself to higher standards than God does?"

"I'm holding myself to the standards of my parents."

"You have strict parents?"

"I have normal parents. But if my parents knew what I did, they wouldn't want me as a son."

Sister Maura nodded as if she understood how he felt. "So you don't plan to tell them what you did."

"No, I don't," he said. "I don't want them to know about it."

"If you told me, I wouldn't tell them."

He was tempted to tell her, but he didn't see how she could help him, so he shook his head, saying: "I'm not ready to talk about it."

"Okay," Sister Maura told him. "But when you're ready, I'll be here for you."

"Thanks, sister. And I'll be prepared for the next class."

"You better be. You have a lot of potential as a student, and I don't want to see you waste it."

That made him feel a little better.

As he was turning to leave, she said: "If you want to talk with a priest, there's a good man at St. Brigid. His name is Father Paul. He came here from Ireland many years ago. He was young when he came here, so he's not too old, and you might feel comfortable talking with him."

"Where is St. Brigid?"

"It's down on Broadway, just south of Roberts Avenue, on the east side of the street."

"Thanks," he said. And he left the classroom.

After his next class, instead of going to the cafeteria for lunch, he went to the spot where they had raped the girl. He stood there and tried to imagine what she had felt. While it was happening he knew from her cries that she had felt pain, but what had she felt when it was over? She must have felt despoiled, stripped of everything that had made her a valued human being. She must have felt like a receptacle for the discharge of excess semen. She must have felt like an object of contempt that was suitable for peeing on. Though it wasn't her fault, she must have felt shame for what had happened to her. So probably the last thing she wanted now was for anyone to know about it.

But if those guys posted the video on a website for gang rapes, then sooner or later someone would identify her, and her defilement would become public. Imagining what she would feel then, he resolved to mitigate the damage.

That afternoon, as they were leaving the field after lacrosse practice, he detached Brandon from the other guys and said: "We need to talk."

"What about?" Brandon asked blithely.

"Kenny told me you have a video of what we did."

"Yeah, I have a video of it. Do you want to watch it?"

"No, I don't. He said you were going to post it on a website."

"I'm thinking about it, but I haven't decided."

"Well, you shouldn't post it on a website."

"Why not? It doesn't show our faces."

"It shows her face."

"It doesn't show her whole face, except at the beginning before we blindfolded her."

"But even blindfolded, she could be identified."

"So she could be identified," Brandon said, twirling his stick as if it were a baton. "But we can't be identified. I mean, unless Scott has a tattoo on his dick that I don't know about."

"If she's identified," Jeffrey said, "then people will know what happened to her."

"I don't care if people know what happened to her."

"You don't care how it would make her feel?"

"Why should I care? She's just a spic."

"She's a human being."

"Oh, don't give me that shit," Brandon said, quickening his pace as if he wanted to get away.

Keeping up with him, Jeffrey changed tactics. "Okay. You don't care how it would make her feel. But if she was identified, she might charge us with rape."

"She can't charge us with anything. She didn't see our faces."

"She heard our voices."

"So what's she going to do? Get the police to record the voice of every guy on campus and try to match them with what she thinks she remembers hearing?"

"She could hear us in the classroom or in the hall."

"I don't have any classes with her, and if I saw her in the hall I wouldn't talk in front of her."

"You might not see her in time to shut up."

"Hey, look," Brandon said, rapping the end of his stick on the pavement. "If you had more experience with girls you'd know they almost never charge guys for rape, abuse, or sexual harassment."

"Why don't they?"

"I don't know. I guess they're afraid to."

"Well, if she was identified in the video, she might not be afraid to charge us. She wouldn't have anything to lose."

"Maybe she wouldn't. But what would she gain by charging us?"

He didn't say justice, he only asked: "What would you gain by posting the video on a website?"

Brandon didn't answer that question, but after thinking about it Jeffrey concluded that it would be a validation of whatever they had gained by raping her.

Later that afternoon he walked down to the Greystone station and took the train to Hastings where he worked at a restaurant on Friday, Saturday, and Sunday evenings. Based on his experience at his father's restaurant, he had gotten a job there as a server, and on good nights, with his share of the tips, he did well. The restaurant was on the waterfront, only a short distance from the Hastings station, so getting there by train was easy.

The restaurant had a large interior space that was supplemented by a patio during the warmer months, and at this time of year it was still warm enough for hardy people to dine on the patio. It also had an extensive bar and two private party rooms. Its prices were high not only because of the items on the menu but also because of the river view. In fact, as one of Jeffrey's co-workers put it, the customers didn't come there for the food, they came there for the view—and to be seen there among people who could afford its prices.

Jeffrey wasn't the only student at St. Catherine who worked at the restaurant. Three other servers were also students at the college, as was the girl who worked as an assistant hostess. Her name was Hailey, and obviously she had gotten her job because of her looks—she was a pretty girl with a smile that made people feel welcome. But she was also a nice girl, as Jeffrey had discovered while talking with her after the evenings started to wind down. Though he liked her, and he could sense that she liked him, as recently as last weekend he had still been working up the courage to ask her out, impeded by the common knowledge that college girls wouldn't have anything to do with freshmen, even if they were freshmen themselves. So he hadn't asked her out, and now he never could.

"Hey, Jeffrey," she said, looking glad to see him.

"Hey," he said abruptly, not stopping to talk with her. He couldn't face her after what he had done. He couldn't look into her pure blue eyes and expose her to whatever had made him pin that girl's arms while three guys raped her.

It was a busy night, so there wasn't another opportunity for them to talk until around ten, when more customers were leaving than arriving.

"Did I do something wrong?" she asked him as they were setting tables for the next day.

"No, you didn't do anything wrong."

"Then why are you avoiding me?"

"I have something on my mind."

"Do you want to talk about it?"

"I can't talk about it."

"You mean you don't want to talk about it?"

"I mean I can't. And anyway it has nothing to do with you."

"Okay," she said, sounding hurt.

"I'm sorry," he said. "I didn't mean it that way. I don't want to talk about it because it would upset you if you knew about it. And I don't want to upset you."

"Are you trying to protect me?"

"Yeah, I'm trying to protect you."

"Well, let me know if you decide that I can handle it."

"I didn't mean you couldn't handle it. I only meant that you shouldn't *have* to handle it."

She nodded. "Okay. I think I understand. It's like not watching one of those videos that shows a guy in black from ISIS cutting off another guy's head."

"Yeah, that's what it's like," he said, impressed by her grasp of the situation.

The next day was Saturday, the day when Catholics traditionally went to confession. Jeffrey hadn't made a confession since shortly after his confirmation, and he was uncertain about his intentions as he walked south on Broadway toward the church that Sister Maura had told him about. Maybe he only wanted to talk with someone about what he had done, but if that was the case, then why hadn't he talked with Sister Maura about it? At least he knew her, and he trusted her. All he knew about this priest was that he'd come from Ireland many years ago, and that Sister Maura said he was a good man.

The church was a small, traditional building with a school next to it and a rectory behind it. Though he knew that few people went to confession anymore, he tried the front door of the church, found it open, and walked in. The church was simple, and the windows were monochrome, functioning only to filter the sunlight. In times past the priest would have been waiting in the confessional for people, and there would have been a line. But the confessional was empty, and Jeffrey wondered if he should have gone instead to the rectory.

Then from the sacristy a priest emerged. As he approached, Jeffrey figured that he was about his father's age, with wavy silver hair and cheery blue eyes.

"Can I help you?" the priest asked him.

"Are you Father Paul?"

"Yes. Who are you?"

"I'm Jeffrey. I'm a student at St. Catherine, and Sister Maura recommended you."

"I'm glad to meet you, Jeffrey," the priest said, extending his hand. They shook hands, and then Father Paul asked: "What did she recommend me for?"

"For someone to talk with."

"Then you're not here for a formal confession?"

"I'm here for a talk, and maybe that's all."

"Then let's sit down," Father Paul said, gesturing toward a rear pew.

Jeffrey slid into the pew first and the priest followed him.

With his body turned and his arm resting casually on the back of the pew, the priest waited for him to begin.

At a loss, Jeffrey wondered if it would have been easier to make a confession since at least he would have known how to begin: "Bless me, father, for I have sinned."

The priest still waited.

"I've done something unforgivable," Jeffrey said with his eyes lowered, unable even to look at the priest.

"That's a strong word. Are we talking about a mortal sin?"

"It's worse than mortal, much worse, but I don't know any other word for it."

"Then tell me about it," Father Paul said gently.

"I play lacrosse at St. Catherine," Jeffrey began, "and after practice on Wednesday, I went with three teammates to a spot off the path that overlooks the river. We were drinking beer, and a girl came walking along the path. She was alone. And one of my teammates grabbed her and carried her to the spot where we were drinking. She was unconscious. I don't know what he did to her, but I guess he choked her. We undressed her, and we raped her."

"You all raped her?"

"All except me. I couldn't do it. But I pinned her arms while the others raped her."

"Then legally you're as guilty as they are."

"I know. And morally I'm as guilty as they are."

Father Paul nodded in agreement. "What happened after they raped her?"

"We tied her hands so she couldn't take off the blindfold until we had a chance to get away."

"You blindfolded her?"

"Yeah, with her shirt. And we gagged her with her panties."

"Ugh. What happened then?"

"We left her there."

"Well, I hope she's not still there."

"No. I went back the next morning, and she wasn't there. She must have untied her hands and dressed and gone back to her dorm."

"You mean she was a student?"

"I assume she was. It happened on the campus."

After a moment the priest asked: "Have you talked with anyone else about it?"

"No. Except with the guys. They made a video of it, and they want to post it on a website. I tried to make our leader understand how she'd feel if they posted the video and someone identified her. But that didn't work. So I tried to make him realize that if the girl was identified, she'd have nothing to lose by charging us with rape. And maybe that worked."

"For the girl's sake, I hope it worked. Is there anything else you want to tell me?"

"Yeah. There is."

The priest waited.

"When I went back to the spot the next morning, I found a silver locket on a chain. I'm sure it belongs to her."

"What's inside the locket?"

"I think it's a picture of Our Lady of Guadalupe?"

"Do you have the locket with you?"

"Yeah." He carefully took it out of his pocket and handed it to the priest.

Father Paul opened the locket and gazed at the picture. "It's Our Lady of Guadalupe. The girl must be Latina."

"She is."

After a silence the priest handed the locket back to him, saying: "I know you're sorry for what you did, but what are you going to do about it?"

"I don't know. That's why I came here."

"Well, I can assign you a penance, and you can say an Act of Contrition, but that won't make your feeling go away."

"I didn't think it would. But what *would* make it go away?"

"A long process of reconciliation could make it go away, and you can start by returning the locket to that girl."

"I intend to return it to her," Jeffrey said. "That's why I kept it. But it'll be hard to return it to her."

"I know," Father Paul said, laying a comforting hand on his shoulder. "But it'll be a lot harder if you don't return it to her."

As a result of this conversation Jeffrey decided to return the locket at the first opportunity. He didn't know the girl's name, and he didn't know where to look for her, so he kept his eyes open for her in the halls, in the library, and in the cafeteria. Every time he saw a Latina, he looked at her closely to see if there was something he remembered from the girl's face, which he had seen in its entirety before they blindfolded her.

The following Tuesday morning he was walking down the hall on his way to a class when he saw a girl whose face had elements that he remembered. She was coming toward him, talking in Spanish with a girl who had big brown eyes. As she drew near, he became certain that it was her, so he moved into her path and said: "Could I talk with you?"

She recoiled as if he had made a lewd remark to her, and then abruptly she turned away and kept walking. The other girl said something to her, and she replied, but he didn't understand what they said because they were talking in Spanish.

Feeling he had blown the opportunity, he decided to try a different approach the next time he saw her. Maybe he would simply offer the locket.

THREE

THOUGH HER BUSINESS ethics class should have started by now, Maura waited another few minutes for the stragglers to arrive. They were usually guys, and sure enough, two big guys sauntered into the classroom with backpacks and lacrosse sticks.

"Brandon and Scott," she told them firmly, "you're twelve minutes late."

"I'm sorry, sister," Brandon said. "We had car trouble."

"Car trouble? You live in the dorm. You can walk from there."

"I didn't mean we drove from there. We were trying to fix my car."

"Well, in the future please don't use class time to fix your car. And please don't bring those sticks to class. You don't need them."

"They *do* need them," a girl said in a loud enough voice. "Those sticks are substitutes for what they're missing."

Most of them laughed, especially the kids who came from urban neighborhoods where they didn't play lacrosse.

Maura had opposed the previous president who believed that adding lacrosse to the college's sports would somehow enhance its reputation. But all it had done was introduce a group of kids who didn't assimilate well with the typical kids who attended St. Catherine because they looked down on them. It also hurt the traditional sports of the college—soccer, baseball, basketball, and volleyball—because it took money away from their budgets to give scholarships to lacrosse players. So Maura had an undeniable bias against lacrosse.

"Okay. Let's settle down. Now, tell us, Brandon, what's the ethical issue in the case about the malaria vaccine?"

"I didn't read that case," Brandon admitted.

"Were you too busy fixing your car?"

"No. I just didn't have time to read it."

"Did you read the other case?"

"No. I didn't have time. We have lacrosse practice every day."

"You have practice Monday through Friday, and it ends at five. You still have the evenings to study, and you have the weekends."

"We go home on weekends."

"You can't study at home?"

"There're a lot of distractions."

"What about you, Scott? Did you read the cases?"

"No, sister. Like Brandon, I didn't have time."

"Well, you guys better start doing the homework, or you're not going to make it."

They looked at her as if they didn't believe her.

"Next week the coach will send me a form to tell him how you're doing, and if I tell him you're not doing the homework, he could suspend you from the team."

"We'll do the homework," Brandon said.

"We will," Scott said.

"You better," Maura said. "Now, tell us, Carla, what's the ethical issue in the case about the malaria vaccine?"

Carla was prepared, and she explained the issue perfectly. Like most of the girls, she did her homework, came to class prepared, and participated in the discussions. The boys were the challenge. They sauntered into the classroom late, they slouched in the back rows, and they tried to get away with using their smartphones during class. Maura had a rule that smartphones weren't allowed during class, and if she caught a student using one, she kicked him out and gave him a failing grade for the day. Needless to say, the kids in her classes rarely tried to use their smartphones, though she could tell that after a while of being deprived of this stimulation they began to suffer from withdrawal symptoms.

The class hadn't started well, but from then on it went well, and when Maura dismissed the students she felt as if she had accomplished something.

She had a full hour to kill before her next class, but instead of going back to her office she went into the faculty lounge and poured herself a mug of coffee, which she drank with half and half. There was no one else in the lounge now, which pleased her since she felt she needed a moment to reflect.

She sat down at a table, with her coffee in front of her, and stared out the window. She had served the college for fifty years—a week ago the new president held a ceremony in Wagner Hall, attended by people who had known Maura for a long time, to celebrate her golden anniversary. She had come to St. Catherine as a young girl to become a nun. She was born and raised on a dairy farm in western New York. The nearest town was Paris, with a population of a few thousand at that time. When people asked her where she was from, especially if she sensed they planned to top her by saying they were from the Bronx, or Brooklyn, or even Inwood, she told them she was from Paris, and then after a long pause added New York.

Since her parents had four sons and five daughters, they had no objection to her becoming a nun. In fact, they supported her decision, as parents of large Irish families with surplus girls often did in that era. After making a lot of inquiries they sent her to the convent of St. Catherine, where she went through the process of becoming a nun under the guidance of Audrey, who was eight years older—still in her twenties then—and like an older sister for her. During the process she did a number of different jobs at the convent, the last of which was running the kitchen. By then she had earned an associate's degree at the college, its only degree at the time, but seeing her potential they sent her to Fordham for her bachelor's degree, and then her master's, and finally her Ph.D. She started teaching right after she got her master's, and since then she had served in every position of the college except one. Though more than once the board of trustees had tried to get her to serve as president, she had always refused, explaining that she didn't have the fund-raising ability required for that position. And now that she was eighty they no longer approached her with that idea.

Of all the jobs she had done at the college, more than anything she liked teaching. She liked being with the students and interacting with them and seeing them learn. By now she had taught three generations of students, which were labeled by sociologists as baby boomers, generation Xers, and millennials. She had noticed the changes from the time when she and Audrey mentored the college's chapter of the Catholic Peace Fellowship which opposed the war in Vietnam to the present day when, without Audrey, she mentored a college organization which helped students deal with issues of race, ethnicity, and gender. In her view, the biggest differences between the baby boomers and the millennials were the latter generation's need for security and their avoidance of confrontation, whereas the baby boomers took risks and challenged authority at every level. She remembered going to the library the day after Hurricane Sandy, when the college was closed and there was no electricity in most other parts of the city, and finding hundreds of students camped out on the floor. When she asked them what they were doing there, they told her they had come to recharge their phones, which made her realize that for this generation that was the top priority.

Despite the differences, Maura found that it was easier to teach kids who could have been her grandchildren than kids who could have been her children. With the latter there was the tension that existed between parents and children, and even though she was clearly identified not as a parent but as a nun—she wore a habit at that time—the girls sometimes rebelled against her as if she was their mother, and the boys sometimes tried to win her love as if she was their mother, whereas now she no longer felt that tension since they regarded her as their grandmother, and she knew from her own experience that kids had easier relationships with their grandparents than with their parents.

Sipping her coffee, she thought about the boy in her freshman seminar who felt he had done something unforgivable. She could only imagine what it was, and she hoped he had taken her advice and gone to see Paul. She knew he was a lacrosse player, but unlike the others he had never brought his stick to class, and he didn't display an attitude of superiority as the others did. She told herself that she shouldn't generalize about lacrosse players, but as a longtime supporter of athletics at the college she couldn't help resenting the fact that lacrosse was being favored over other sports, even though the president who had brought it to the college had moved on. The fact that lacrosse players came from middle to upper income families, who lived in suburbs where they played the sport, conflicted with the mission of the college, which was to provide a high-quality education for students who couldn't otherwise afford it. Most of the kids at the undergraduate level were from poor families and lived in urban neighborhoods where they played sports on the streets.

At that moment she was joined in the lounge by Solana, the youngest nun, who hadn't yet turned forty. Her parents were from the Dominican Republic, and she was born and raised in the Bronx, near the high school that the sisters had established. In fact, her father had worked as custodian of the high school until his retirement a few years ago. Solana decided to become a nun after her fiancé was killed in a fight to protect her from a gang who attacked her. It happened in Manhattan, not in the Bronx, and it sent her into an abyss from which only her faith lifted her. Being bilingual, she was a valuable asset for the college since more than forty percent of its students spoke Spanish.

"Do you mind if I join you?" Solana asked, stopping at her table with a mug of coffee.

"Not at all," Maura said. "At this point I need company."

"Why do you need company?" Solana asked, sitting down.

"Oh, I was thinking about lacrosse, and I need to complain to someone about it."

"You do? So complain to me about it."

"Okay. I have two lacrosse players in my business ethics class who as usual arrived late this morning, and as usual brought their sticks to class."

"They do that with me, though I keep asking them not to bring their sticks with them."

"A girl put them down with an apt remark. She said the sticks are substitutes for what they're missing."

Solana laughed. "I agree with her. I've always thought they carry their sticks around the campus to prove they're *macho*."

"But I have a lacrosse player who's different, so I shouldn't generalize about them."

"I have one too. He's in my religion class. His name is Jeffrey."

"That's the name of the kid I was talking about. He has brown hair, brown eyes, and he looks very young for his age?"

"Yeah, it's the same kid."

"Well, he's in my freshman seminar, and he was doing well, but last Friday he had a meltdown."

Solana was attentive.

"I wanted to know what was wrong, so I asked him to stay after class, and I got him to talk about it. He told me he did something unforgivable."

"Unforgivable?"

"He wouldn't tell me what it was, so I advised him to go and see Paul."

"That's interesting," Solana said, "because in my class yesterday we had a discussion about forgiveness."

"Did he participate in the discussion?"

"Yeah. He said he believed that some actions are unforgivable, and that there's no way we can ever atone for them."

"Whatever he did, he sure feels guilty about it."

"At his age what could he have done?"

"I don't know. Maybe he betrayed someone," Maura suggested, knowing how much the kids valued loyalty.

"Or hurt someone physically."

"Yeah. That's possible." She had viewed the results of an act of violence when two lacrosse players had come before the disciplinary committee for breaking furniture in a student lounge, and she could imagine whatever had impelled them to destroy property being turned against a person.

"When I see those guys together," Solana said in a subdued voice, "I think about what guys in gangs are capable of doing."

"Well, I hope he took my advice and talked with Paul about it. I believe he's a good kid, and I don't want to lose him."

"If he's sorry for what he did, then there's hope for him."

In her next class, the freshman seminar, Maura wanted to give her undivided attention to the students in front of her, so she put Jeffrey out of her mind for a while, but her concern for him was replaced by her concern for Esperanza, who had missed the class last Thursday. She was a Latina, who from the beginning had sat in the middle of the front row, eager to learn. But today she sat in the desk that was nearest the door as if she wanted to be in a position to escape. It wasn't only that she had missed the last class and had shifted out of her usual position, it was also the look in her dark eyes. It was the look of someone who had lost all hope for the land of the living and wanted to die.

When Maura called on her during the discussion, the girl admitted that she hadn't done the assignment, so she left her alone until the end of the class, and then she asked her to stay for a moment. The girl had already jumped up and was heading for the door, but she stopped and stood there as if she had done something wrong and expected to be punished for it.

Waiting until all of the other students had left the classroom, Maura closed the door and said: "You were absent last Thursday, and you weren't mentally here today."

"I'm sorry, sister," the girl said in a low voice.

She led the girl to the desk where some professors sat while conducting classes.

Walking alongside Esperanza, she realized that the girl was only about five feet two and couldn't weigh more than ninety pounds. Though not a big woman herself, she felt she could have lifted the girl and cradled her. She sat on the edge of the desk, which brought their heads to about the same level. "Are you all right?"

The girl shook her head, fighting tears.

"Would you like to talk about it?"

The girl again shook her head.

"Did something happen to a member of your family?"

"No." A tear escaped from one of the girl's eyes, and with one of her hands she quickly stopped it from traveling farther.

"Did something happen to you?"

The girl took a gulp of air that precluded her from answering the question but indicated that something *had* happened to her.

"What was it?" Maura asked gently.

"It was nothing," the girl finally said, pulling herself together. "It was just an accident."

"What kind of accident?"

"I wasn't prepared for my period, and I messed up my jeans."

Maura couldn't accept this story since it didn't explain the obvious depth of the girl's misery. It was the kind of story a girl would tell her mother to hide what had really happened. "Are you sure that's all?"

"Yeah, that's all," the girl insisted.

"Well, if you're in any kind of trouble, you can always talk with me about it. You can come to my office in Farrell Hall, where we'll have complete privacy."

The girl looked as if she was afraid that Maura had guessed what kind of trouble she was in, and she retorted: "I'm not pregnant, if that's what you think."

"I don't think anything. I only want you to know that whatever kind of trouble you're in, you can safely talk with me about it."

"I'm not in any kind of trouble," the girl said as if that was the end of it.

"Okay. Then I'll see you on Thursday."

Maura watched the girl leave the classroom, walking as if there was a heavy weight on her shoulders. She knew that something had happened to her, and from the girl's denial that she was pregnant she had an inkling of what it was.

As she walked across the campus to her office Maura was bothered by something in the girl's appearance today. It wasn't her clothes since she wore the usual jeans and shirt. Like most of the other Latina girls she didn't show cleavage, which now was all the rage for white girls, but some of the Latina girls wore jeans so tight you wondered how they got into them. Esperanza's jeans fit her snugly, but they weren't especially tight. You could tell that she was well raised, or *bien educada* as they said in their language. From a writing exercise she had given her students in the first class, Maura remembered that the girl's parents had emigrated from Mexico, and that they regularly attended mass at San Pedro, where the congregation was mostly Latino. And she wore a chain around her neck with a silver locket at the end of it.

Coming to a halt, Maura realized what she was bothered by. She recalled the girl standing near her, and she was sure of it: the girl wasn't wearing the locket today. Now, maybe she had only forgotten to put it on this morning, or maybe she had mislaid it, or maybe she had decided to stop wearing it because she had lost her faith in what the locket stood for. Given the look of despair in her eyes, the last possibility seemed the most likely. But what had made her lose her faith? Whatever had happened, it wasn't just an accident.

That afternoon she was in her office at Farrell Hall, where the school of liberal arts was located. For her years of service they had given her one of the two private offices in the building, with the other one going to the dean. She made use of the privacy for talking with students, usually about their academic problems but also about their family problems, their financial problems, and their personal problems. The government bureaucrats who saw only the numbers couldn't understand why it took six years for the average student to get through college, but if you knew what the students were up against in their lives, you felt it was a miracle that they got through college at all. There were so many things that could stop them from continuing, from the loss of a job to the breakup of a family to the uncovered expense of an illness. Most of them lived at the edge of financial disaster, and they had suffered the full brunt of the recent recession.

She was grading the weekly papers she assigned to her students, which was one of her least favorite activities, and whenever students complained about having to write so many papers she reminded them that she had to grade them. She had just corrected a common grammatical error when the student worker at the reception desk phoned and told her there was a student who wanted to see her. Without asking the student's name, she agreed to see whoever it was, and she got up, welcoming relief from the chore of grading papers.

She wasn't surprised that it was Jeffrey, who had a look of desperation in his eyes. She ushered him into her office and closed the door and invited him to sit down in the chair next to her desk. She turned so that they were facing each other over a corner of her desk, and she asked: "Did you talk with Father Paul?"

"Yeah." The boy swallowed as if there was a lump in his throat. "He gave me some advice, which I tried to follow."

"What was the advice?"

Jeffrey reached into the pocket of his jeans and drew out something and laid it on her desk. It was a silver locket on a broken chain. "He said I should return this locket."

"Who does it belong to?"

"It belongs to a girl in your freshman seminar, the section that meets on Tuesdays and Thursdays."

"How did you get it?"

"She lost it, and I found it."

"When did you find it?"

"Last Thursday."

"Why didn't you return it right away?"

"I didn't know who it belonged to."

"How did you find out who it belonged to?"

"I recognized her in the hall."

"So you don't know her?"

"No, I don't know her."

"If you don't know her, then how do you know she's in my freshman seminar?"

"I followed her there."

"Then why didn't you return it to her?"

"I tried to return it, but she wouldn't talk with me."

"This isn't making sense. You have to tell me more about it."

He shook his head. "I don't want to talk about it."

"Then why did you come here?"

"To ask a favor."

"A favor?"

"Yeah. I want you to return the locket to her."

"But why can't *you* return it to her?"

"I just can't face her."

Maura was connecting the pieces and beginning to imagine what might have happened. "Is she the one you did something unforgivable to?"

The boy nodded, closing his eyes.

"What did you do to her?"

"I'm sorry, but I can't tell you."

"Did you tell Father Paul?"

"Yeah. I told him."

"And he advised you to return the locket?"

"That's right."

"When you approached her, did you tell her what you were trying to do?"

"No. I didn't get that far. She turned away from me, and she kept walking. She was with a friend, which made it harder."

"You mean harder to talk with her?"

"Yeah." Jeffrey gazed sorrowfully at the locket as if it was testimony against him.

After reflecting, Maura asked: "Why do you think Father Paul advised you to return the locket?"

"I don't know. I guess he wanted me to talk with her. But if she won't talk with me, what can I do?"

"You can try again."

"I guess I can, but what if she still won't talk with me?"

"If she knows you have her locket, she might talk with you."

"But she might not, and I want her to have it, so if you return it then she'll have it."

"And you'll avoid having to face her."

Jeffrey shook his head, saying: "You don't understand."

"No, I don't. But I might understand if you told me what you did to her."

"Just take my word for it. What I did to her was unforgivable."

"All right. I'll take your word for it. But if I return the locket to her, then you might not have another chance for reconciliation with her."

With a look of utter despair he asked: "How could there ever be reconciliation? How could she ever forgive me?"

"I don't know. But unless she forgives you, she might never recover from what you did to her. So instead of just thinking about yourself, you should think about *her*."

That seemed to make an impression on him, and after a silence he reached for the locket, saying: "Okay. I'll try again."

That evening after dinner she felt a need to share her thoughts with someone who had more experience outside the convent, so she invited Solana to her room, where they could talk without any risk of being overheard by a nosy nun. Since her room was small, Solana sat in the only chair while Maura sat on the edge of her bed and recounted her conversations with Esperanza and Jeffrey.

When she had finished, Solana said: "So he wouldn't tell you what he did to her."

"No. He told Paul, but he wouldn't tell me."

"Maybe he wouldn't tell you because you're a woman."

"What does that have to do with it?"

"As a woman you might judge him more severely. I mean, he might have done to her what those guys would have done to me."

Remembering how the girl had denied that she was pregnant, Maura said: "You mean he might have assaulted her?"

"He might have, though I must admit that he doesn't seem like the kind of guy who would do such a thing."

"He doesn't at all."

"But if he was with several other guys, and if he felt pressure to go along with them, I can imagine him doing such a thing. I know what guys in gangs are capable of doing."

"He plays lacrosse," Maura said, "so those guys are his buddies. He could have gone along with them in assaulting Esperanza."

"Well, if they assaulted her, we have a lot of issues to deal with."

"Yeah, we do. But our top priority should be to bring about a reconciliation between Jeffrey and Esperanza."

Solana frowned. "Do you think that's possible?"

"Anything's possible. So we should give them a chance to talk with each other before we get into a process."

"But sooner or later we'll have to get into a process. If those guys assaulted her, we don't want them here as students."

"We certainly don't," Maura agreed. "But according to our policy we can't make the girl report what they did to her, we can only advise her to report it."

"Who would she report it to?"

"She could report it to our Title IX coordinator, or report it to me as head of the disciplinary committee."

"You'd want her to report it to you, wouldn't you?"

"Yeah, I would," Maura said, believing that she could help Esperanza in her role as head of the committee.

"If the girl was assaulted," Solana said, "and if our committee found those guys guilty, what could we do to them?"

"We could expel them."

"We couldn't do anything more to them?"

"No. If the case went to court, and if a jury found them guilty, a judge could do a lot more to them."

"But you wouldn't want the case to go to court."

"No, I wouldn't," Maura said. "I wouldn't want the girl to go through that ordeal."

"So you'll advise her to report it?"

"I will eventually. But first I want her to talk with Jeffrey. I want to give them a chance to start the process of reconciliation."

After a silence Solana said: "You know, it's not a simple matter of her forgiving him. Jeffrey has to forgive himself. They both have to stop blaming themselves."

"Why would the girl blame herself?"

"I can't explain why, but that's how you feel after it happens. You feel it was your fault."

"Did you feel it was your fault that those guys attacked you?"

"Yeah, I did. So I felt it was my fault that Rafael got killed defending me."

"Then you can understand how Esperanza feels, and you can help her, especially since you can talk with her in Spanish."

"Well, before I start trying to help her, I need to know what happened to her."

"If you asked her, she might tell you."

Solana shook her head. "If she knew we talked about it, then she might not trust either of us. So I don't think I should get involved yet."

"All right. I'll advise Jeffrey to keep trying to return the locket. It's the only reason she might have for talking with him."

"So was it a blessing that he found the locket?"

"I wouldn't call it a blessing yet," Maura said. "If he doesn't do the right thing with it, the locket could end up being a curse. So let's see what he does with it."

FOUR

"*LO CONOCES?*" Griselda asked as they resumed walking and left the guy behind them.

"No. I never saw him before," Esperanza said truthfully. She never saw him, but she thought she recognized his voice. It was the voice of the guy who had pinned her arms.

"I wonder what he wanted."

"I don't know, and I don't care." Whatever it was, it could only make things worse for her. She was afraid he would expose her and let the whole world know what they had done to her, so she hoped she never saw him again.

They parted when they got to the room where Griselda had her next class, and Esperanza continued walking, debating whether to cut her freshman seminar. She had cut the last class to avoid facing the professor, an old nun who was very observant and just from looking at her might be able to guess what had happened to her.

But cutting two classes in a row would raise a red flag. The professor would send a message to Esperanza's advisor, who would want to meet with her and find out what the problem was, and she wanted even less to talk with her advisor than with the professor, who as a nun at least could be trusted to maintain the shelter of confidentiality. So she went into the classroom and sat at a desk near the door, where she had a quick avenue of escape in case the professor tried to ask her to stay after class.

The subject of the course was ethics, and for every class they had an assignment to read a case study and write about an ethical issue raised by the situation. Then in class they discussed the situation and they shared what they had written about it. Until last week Esperanza had been doing well in the course, but she hadn't done the assignment for today, which gave her an additional reason to avoid facing the professor.

As the class began, Esperanza kept a low profile, hoping to stay out of the professor's line of vision, and for a while she succeeded. But then the professor called on her, and she had to admit that she hadn't done the assignment. The professor looked disappointed but didn't call on her again, and Esperanza wasn't distracted from the scenarios that played out in her mind.

In the worst scenario she was pregnant and she had to deal with the issue of whether or not to have the baby. Of course in her religion having an abortion was strictly forbidden, and it was at the top of the list of mortal sins. So she couldn't seriously consider an abortion, though she could consider one of those pills that you take the morning after having sex. But now it was six days later, probably too late, and she wished she had thought of this sooner. She wished she knew someone with experience who could give her advice on what to do.

Assuming she had the baby, she would then have to deal with the issue of whether or not to keep it. If she kept the baby, it would rule out going to college, at least for a while, and that would make her father unhappy. She knew that being the first born she was his treasure, his gift from God, and it would hurt him deeply to learn what had happened to her. She had never seen him angry, but she could imagine how he would react, and she was afraid he would do something that would hurt him even more. So she reconsidered having an abortion. He didn't have to know about it, and if he didn't know, it wouldn't hurt him.

But how did you arrange to have an abortion? Did you go to the doctor who treated your family? Did you go to the emergency room? And how could you pay for an abortion without your parents finding out about it?

She decided to try taking that pill for the morning after and hope it wasn't too late.

At the end of the class the professor asked her to stay for a moment, and when they were alone the professor asked her if she was all right.

Softened by the professor's concern for her, she came close to revealing what had happened. But she was stopped by her doubt that this celibate old woman could even imagine what it was like to be gang-raped and peed on. So she told her the lie she had told her mother.

Later, as she was hanging out in Griselda's room, she said to her friend: "*Tengo una pregunta.* Do you know anything about the pill you take the morning after having sex?"

"Why are you asking?" Griselda said, looking worried.

"A girl in my freshman seminar asked me where she could get one, and I didn't know."

"Well, you can get one at a drugstore."

"Do you need a prescription?"

"No, if you're eighteen or older. Just for the record," Griselda added, "I've never had sex, and I only know about that pill from my older sister."

"There are times when I wish I had an older sister."

"Sometimes it's useful to have one."

"I've never had sex either," Esperanza said truthfully. What had happened to her wasn't sex, it was violence. "So you have to take the pill the morning after?"

"It's most effective if you do. The longer you wait, the less effective the pill is. It doesn't take long for one of those creatures to find an egg."

"Did your sister ever get pregnant?"

"No, but she needed that pill more than once. She's on the other pill now."

"Could you ask her for the name of the pill she used?"

"Yeah, sure." Griselda looked at her closely.

"It's not for me, it's for that girl in my freshman seminar."

"Okay. I'll text my sister."

Esperanza watched while Griselda texted her sister, feeling a little bad about using her friend this way. But she would be happy to let Griselda use her the same way.

Within five minutes Griselda got a reply from her sister, and she held out her smartphone to Esperanza so that she could read the name of the pill.

Esperanza copied it into her phone and pretended to send a message to the imaginary girl.

Since it was Tuesday, one of her father's two days off, she was expected home for dinner by six thirty. Her mother always cooked dinner for the family, giving her father a break from cooking at the restaurant.

Esperanza left the dormitory with enough time to make a stop on the way home. She got off the bus at Roberts Avenue and walked to Palisade Avenue, where there was a drugstore that Griselda went to for supplies. She didn't want to go to the drugstore in her neighborhood since the people who worked there knew her, and they would take note of what she was buying. It might even get back to her mother.

Though the guy behind the counter didn't know her and would probably never see her again, she still felt self-conscious asking him for the pill, but he got it for her without comment as if he was used to girls asking for it.

She bought a bottle of spring water, and as she walked back to Broadway to catch a bus for the remainder of her trip home, she opened the package and took a pill, which she washed down with the water. At the corner she dropped the package into a trashcan, destroying the evidence. And she prayed that it wasn't too late.

At home she found her mother in the kitchen, which was the room nearest the entrance to their apartment. From the sounds coming from the living room, she assumed that her father was watching Mexican *fútbol* on television, probably with her brother.

"*Cómo van tus clases?*" her mother asked, taking a tortilla out of the pan with her fingers.

"*Van bien*," she replied dutifully.

"You need to do well to keep your scholarship."

"I know," she said, wishing her mother would stop reminding her of this.

After slipping the last tortilla into the container that kept them warm, her mother wiped her hands on her apron and came over and hugged her as if to make up for nagging her.

She responded to the hug, needing it.

"Are you all right?" her mother asked her, looking directly into her eyes.

"I'm fine," she insisted.

"What happened to your locket?"

"I don't know." She always removed the locket before going to sleep and before taking a shower. "I looked around my bed, and I looked in the bathroom, but I couldn't find it."

"Did you take it off at school?"

"No. I only take it off at home."

"Then it must be around here somewhere."

"I'm sure it is. I'll keep looking for it." She hated lying to her mother, but the only alternative was to tell the truth, which she absolutely couldn't do.

"If the clasp broke," her mother said, "it could have fallen off."

"Oh, I would have noticed."

"I hope you would have. You kids don't pay attention to what's happening around you when you're on your phones."

"Don't worry. I'm not going to walk in front of a bus."

"*Que Dios te proteja.* Please go and tell your father that dinner's ready."

Glad to escape from the watchful eyes of her mother, she went into the living room, where she found her father and Charro cheering. Their team had scored a goal, which was being replayed over and over.

"*Qué golazo!*" her father exclaimed. He gave her a hug that strongly combined his joy at the goal and his love for her.

She pressed her face against his chest, feeling safe in his arms. It occurred to her that this was the only place where she would ever feel safe again. But what if he found out what had happened to her? Would he still hug her? Would he still love her?

"*Mi tesoro,*" he said, kissing her head. "I thank God for you every day."

She was fighting tears, not wanting her father to see them. But when they separated from the hug, he noticed that her eyes were wet, and he asked: "*Estás bien?*"

"Yeah. I'm fine. I'm just happy."

"You make us all happy."

Wiping her eyes with the back of her hand, she delivered the message: "Dinner's ready."

"There're only five minutes left in the match," Charro said.

"Our family's more important than *fútbol*," their father told him. "Your mother's waiting for us. *Vamos, chico.*"

Somehow she got through the next two days, and on Friday she didn't have any classes, so she didn't have to go to the college. Instead, she had to go to work at a Dominican restaurant on South Broadway, just south of the hospital. Her mother ate lunch there once or twice a week, interrupting the routine of the hospital cafeteria, and she had gotten to know the owners, who also attended San Pedro. Soon after Esperanza turned eighteen her mother helped her get a job at the restaurant serving people who used the buffet and took out food. She worked there for five hours on Friday, Saturday, and Sunday, earning the minimum wage but also getting a share of the tips. So she had money to buy clothes, cosmetics, and hair products.

The food at the buffet included grilled chicken, roast pork, beans, rice, and plantains. The beans were pink, and they were soupy, unlike the refried beans that Mexicans ate, but after several months of working at the restaurant and getting free lunches, Esperanza preferred the way Dominicans cooked beans. She had also acquired a taste for *sancocho*, a Dominican stew that had everything in it.

The customers were mostly from the neighborhood and from the hospital. The nursing assistants, nurses, and doctors were dressed in their different colored scrubs, and many of them knew Esperanza's mother, so they tipped her well.

As a nice doctor dropped a folded bill into the jar, she

wondered what he would think of her if he found out what had happened to her. Would he think it had somehow been her fault?

For the hundredth time she told herself that it hadn't been her fault. She had done nothing to attract those guys. She had simply been walking along the path, in proper attire, when one of them grabbed her from behind. He couldn't have seen her face before he attacked her. All he had seen was her body from behind, and her jeans weren't anywhere near as tight as the jeans that some of the other girls wore. So it wasn't her fault.

But even though they had blindfolded her, gagged her, and immobilized her, she still felt that somehow it *was* her fault that three guys had sex with her, one after another. And if these people from the hospital found out about it, they would regard her mother with contempt for raising a daughter who had turned out to be a *puta*.

Again she told herself that they wouldn't find out. She wasn't going to tell anyone, and those guys wouldn't tell anyone since what they had done to her was a crime, and they could go to prison for it. So she was safe—unless she was pregnant. She had another week before she was due for her period, and then she would know if her prayers had been answered or if that pill had worked. In the meantime she could only keep praying and counting the days.

On Sunday she went to church as usual with her family. The church had a mass in Spanish at ten o'clock. It was on Riverdale Avenue, only a few blocks away from the building where they lived, so they could walk there in less than ten minutes, but her mother liked to get there early in order to get their usual places in the fifth pew on the left side, at the middle aisle, so they left the apartment by nine thirty.

They walked along Ludlow Street with her mother and Esperanza ahead and her father and Charro behind at a distance that increased as they advanced toward Riverdale Avenue. The church was on the corner, with walls of gray stone and beautiful stained-glass windows. It dated to a time when the neighborhood was wealthier.

Her father caught up with them in time to open the front door and hold it for her mother, who always led the way into the church. When they reached their pew, her mother genuflected and made the sign of the cross, and then occupied a position that left room for the rest of her family. She always knelt and prayed for a while, and her family followed her example, and then she settled back and waited for the procession, gazing upward with solemn eyes at the figure of Christ nailed to the cross.

Esperanza's prayers before the mass were usually to give thanks for her family, for her life, and for the privilege of going to college, among other things. But today she didn't feel thankful for anything. In fact, she felt that God had forsaken her. She also continued to feel that what had happened to her was somehow her fault, so she was both a victim and a sinner at the same time, though being in church made her feel more like a sinner.

When the priest gave the initial blessing, she crossed herself along with everyone else in the church, but she felt as if she didn't belong there. She went through the motions of following the mass, but when the time approached for Communion she felt she really *was* unworthy to receive the sacrament, and she doubted that her soul could ever be healed.

She was in her usual position, next to her father, who was at the aisle, with her brother on her left, and feeling soiled, she had decided not to join her family in receiving Communion. But then she realized that if she didn't go with them, her mother would wonder what she had done that made her feel unworthy of receiving communion. So she finally got up and waited in the aisle for her mother to lead the way.

"*El Cuerpo de Cristo*," the priest said, placing the Host into her cupped hands. As she tried to put it into her mouth her hands were shaking, and she was afraid that she would drop it. She had no idea what you were supposed to do if you dropped the Host, but luckily she got it into her mouth, turning from the priest and crossing herself.

Luckily her mother was so involved with God that she didn't notice anything unusual.

On Monday after her math class she was on her way to the cafeteria when out of nowhere a girl stopped her and urgently said: "We need to talk."

The girl was a head taller than her, with pulled-back hair, a long face, and intense blue eyes.

"I don't know you," she stammered, feeling as she had when that boy stopped her.

"My name is Wendy," the girl said. "Do you have a class now?"

"No. I'm going to the cafeteria for lunch."

"I have pizza in my room. Come on, let's go there."

Wendy put an arm around her and turned her back in the other direction. She didn't want to go with this girl, but for some reason she was in her power.

"You're Esperanza Vargas, right?" the girl said as they left the building.

"How do you know me?"

"From your picture in Facebook."

She had posted a profile on Facebook when she was in high school, along with every other girl her age. But she hardly went there anymore, feeling that she had outgrown it.

"You look younger in that picture, but you haven't changed much."

As they headed toward the dormitory Esperanza asked: "Can you tell me what this is about?"

"I will as soon as we have some privacy."

They didn't talk again until they were in Wendy's room. It was on the same floor of the dormitory as Griselda's room, which reassured Esperanza. If anything happened, she could run down the hall and get help from her friend.

The room was dominated by a desktop computer whose screen was almost as large as the television screen in the student lounge.

"Please sit down," Wendy said, motioning toward one of the two chairs.

Esperanza sat down, wondering if this girl watched movies on her computer. As well as playing games on his computer, Charro watched movies.

"I know what those guys did to you," Wendy said without a preamble.

"What do you mean?" Esperanza asked, hoping it wasn't what she thought it was.

"I know they raped you."

"Oh, my God." She held her hand against her mouth as if to stop herself from throwing up. "How did you find out?"

"They made a video of the whole thing, which they posted on a website for gang rapes."

"A video? Then everyone will know about it."

"Everyone doesn't watch videos of gang rapes," Wendy said. "But people who watch it will tell other people about it, and it'll go viral."

"Dios, por qué has hecho esto a mí?"

"I don't know why. You're a good girl, and you did nothing to deserve it."

"You understand Spanish?"

"I spent a year in a *barrio* in Los Angeles doing social work."

Trying to pull herself together, Esperanza asked: "How did you find out about the video?"

"I monitor those websites for the purpose of identifying guys who commit gang rape."

"Does the video show their faces?"

"No, they were careful about that. But they made the mistake of showing your face before they gagged and blindfolded you." Wendy reached for something and handed her a photo that showed her lying on her back unconscious.

Esperanza looked at the picture. They hadn't yet undressed her, but she knew what followed, and she covered her eyes to block it out.

"I got that picture from the video. It's definitely you."

"No me queda nada por qué vivir."

"I don't agree. You do have something to live for."

"What?" Ahead of her she could see only a bleak future of mortification and disgrace.

"Bringing those guys to justice."

"I don't want to bring them to justice. I want to go back to what I was before."

"You can't go back. You have to go forward."

"But I didn't see their faces," she argued, "and if the video doesn't show their faces, how would you identify them?"

"Did you hear their voices?"

She had definitely heard their voices, but she didn't want to admit it. She didn't want to get caught up in this girl's mission. "I might have, but I don't remember them."

"I think you do remember them."

She was conscious of the guy who had stopped her in the hall. She remembered his voice when he had said he didn't want to do it. To buy more time to think about it, she asked: "Why did you tell me about the video?"

"I wanted you to know about it, so you'd be prepared. And I wanted you to join my mission to stop the violence against women on college campuses."

"Why is that your mission?"

"Like you, I was a victim of it. Before I went and did social work," Wendy explained, "I was a student at a big university. You know, with fraternity houses. And I went to a party at one of the houses. I had a few drinks, but I didn't get drunk, and I didn't invite them to carry me up to a room and tie my hands and feet to the posts of a bed and rape me. I lost count after the fifth, but there were a lot of them."

"Did they blindfold you?"

"No. They didn't care if I saw their faces. And they didn't gag me, so I could scream. But no one came to help me."

"I'm sorry," Esperanza said, feeling the pain of the other girl.

"I went to the dean of students. I had their names, and I could positively identify them. But they were football players, so the college didn't want to touch them. I had a hearing, but the verdict was that I'd consented to what they did." With a bitter laugh

Wendy added: "Can you imagine a girl consenting to have sex with all those guys?"

"So what did you do then?"

"I went to the police. But that was more than a week later, and they didn't find any evidence of rape, so they didn't take me seriously."

"Did people on campus know what had happened?"

"Oh, yeah. They didn't make a video of it, but they made sure that everyone knew. And I couldn't bear the way guys looked at me when I walked by them, so I dropped out."

"Did you feel it was your fault?"

"Of course I did. We're programmed to feel it's our fault if anything like that happens. Somehow we asked for it."

"But you didn't ask for it, and I didn't either."

"I know. There's no logic to it."

"Do you still feel it was your fault?"

"No, I got over that. And you will too," Wendy added.

After a silence Esperanza said: "I don't know what I can do to help you."

"I'm not asking you to help me. I'm asking you to help yourself by bringing those guys to justice."

"Well, I don't see how that would help me."

"It would help the cause of all women."

"But what if the same thing happened to me? What if the college didn't want to touch those guys? And what if the police didn't take me seriously?"

"That's a risk, but if we build a good case, we can win it. And there are differences between this college and that university."

"What are they?"

"This college doesn't depend so much on sports for its reputation. In fact, it doesn't have a football team. So if those guys are athletes, it won't be afraid to touch them. And this college is committed to Catholic values," Wendy continued, "whereas that university isn't committed to any values, except for its national ranking, which isn't affected by the number of sexual assaults on campus."

"But we don't have any evidence against those guys."

"We have the video, and I have to believe there's something in it that will identify them."

"I can't think about bringing them to justice," Esperanza said. "I'm too worried about being pregnant."

"Have you had your period since it happened?"

"No. I should have my period in a week or so, but if I'm pregnant, I don't know what I'm going to do."

"You could have an abortion."

"I couldn't have an abortion. It's against my religion."

"I know, but under the circumstances—"

"I'm not going to have an abortion."

"Okay. But if you change your mind, I can help you get one without your parents finding out."

"Did you get pregnant?"

Wendy nodded. "It's against my religion to have an abortion, but when I thought about having a baby with the defective genes from one of those monsters, I was able to justify it. And I have no regrets about it. Babies should be conceived in love."

"I hope I don't have to make that decision."

"I hope you don't. But if you don't care about bringing those guys to justice, let me tell you one more thing about the video. I watched it from beginning to end, and you know what the leader did before they left you?"

"No," she lied, not wanting to admit it.

"He peed on you. He treated you like a urinal, like a plumbing fixture. And if you let him get away with it, you'll lose all human dignity as a woman."

"The video shows him doing that?"

"Yeah. There was no sound, but I could imagine them laughing about it."

"They *were* laughing," she confirmed. "They were laughing like it was the funniest thing they'd ever seen."

"Then you should want to bring them to justice."

"Maybe I do. But right now it's not my top priority."

"I understand. You need to find out if you're pregnant."

"Yeah. Well, I have to go. I have a class."

As she left the dormitory she wanted to believe that Wendy was an angel sent by God to help her, but she had doubts about joining her mission. Still, she was grateful for being alerted to the video. If it went viral, then every student would know what had happened to her, and she would have to drop out of the college, as Wendy had dropped out of the university. But first she had to find out if she was pregnant. And it occurred to her that she might be able to find out sooner by taking a pregnancy test before her period was due.

After her class she texted Griselda, who replied that she was in her room, so she went back to the dormitory. Griselda's door was open, and after a knock to signal her arrival Esperanza went in. Griselda must have been studying since there was an open textbook on her desk and a notebook with a pen lying on it.

"*Lo siento. No te interrumpo?*" Esperanza said.

"*No hay problema.* I need a break. This stuff is boring."

"Are you working on your English course?"

"Yeah. We're reading essays."

Esperanza had placed at a higher level than Griselda and was reading poems for her English course. She liked some of them, but she had trouble understanding others. She sat down in the other chair after Griselda had removed her clothes from it. And then she said: "I have another question. What do you know about pregnancy tests?"

"I don't know anything about them. But my sister does."

"I need to know if you have to miss your period before you can take one."

Griselda looked at her closely. "You mean the girl in your freshman seminar needs to know?"

"She keeps asking me questions, and I don't have the answers."

"Well, I can get the answers from my sister. She's taken a lot of pregnancy tests."

"Has she ever gotten pregnant?"

"No. *Gracias a Dios.*" Griselda texted her sister. It took her a while to write the message, typing with her thumbs. And it took a while for her sister to respond.

Esperanza leaned forward anxiously.

"She says you can take a pregnancy test as early as four days before your period is due, but it might give you a false negative."

"But if it was positive, you could believe it?"

Griselda texted something and waited. "Yeah, if it was positive, you could believe it. But if you want to rule out being pregnant, you have to wait until your period is due."

"You mean until you have your period."

Griselda texted again and waited. "She says that if you wait at least two weeks after you're supposed to ovulate, and if the test is negative, then you can believe it, even if you haven't started your period. It could be late for another reason."

"Okay. Thanks." She lingered, feeling that if she got up right away Griselda would think she had come to see her only to get an answer to her question, and though it had been her primary reason, it hadn't been her only reason. She liked Griselda, and she valued her friendship, so she hoped their relationship wouldn't be affected by what had happened to her.

"You know, if you're in trouble," Griselda said after a silence, "you can tell me about it."

"I'm not in trouble," Esperanza insisted. "I'm only trying to help that girl."

Griselda just looked at her.

Esperanza reconsidered. She could see that if the video of what those guys had done to her went viral, and if Griselda found out about it from someone else, then she would be hurt by Esperanza's unwillingness to confide in her. She would feel that Esperanza didn't trust her, and without trust there could be no relationship. So she finally said: "Okay. I *am* in trouble. I think I might be pregnant."

"I didn't know you had a boyfriend."

"I don't have a boyfriend. I was raped by three guys."

"*Dios mio,*" Griselda said, bringing her hands against her mouth.

"They attacked me while I was walking on the path that overlooks the river. One of them grabbed me from behind and choked me, and I lost consciousness. The next thing I knew they were holding me down and raping me, taking turns."

"*Lo siento mucho*," Griselda said with tears in her eyes. "When you came here last week to use the shower, I had a feeling it was more than just an accident, but I never imagined anything like that."

"I'm sorry I didn't tell you then, but—"

"I understand. I wouldn't have wanted to tell anyone."

"So that's why I wanted to know about the pill for the morning after, and why I wanted to know about pregnancy tests."

"I hope you're not pregnant, but what if you are? What will you do?"

"I haven't decided. There are no good choices."

They were silent for a while, facing those choices, and then Griselda asked: "Are you going to bring charges against those guys?"

"I don't know who they are. I didn't see their faces. They blindfolded me."

"*Malditos cabrones! Deben tener sus penes cortados!*"

Esperanza was moved by this burst of anger. It not only made her realize how much Griselda cared about her, but it also put her in touch with a feeling that had been buried under her shame. With anger she added: "*Y sus cojones también.*"

"Whatever happens, I'll be here for you."

"Thanks. I should warn you, they made a video of what they did to me, and they posted it on a website. So it won't be long before everyone knows about it."

"Why would they post a video of it?"

"I don't know," Esperanza said. "I guess for the same reason that they raped me."

"You mean to humiliate you."

"From what I heard, the video even shows what they did before they left me."

"What did they do before they left you?"

"*El líder hizo pis en mí.*"

"*Qué barbaridad!*"

"So the pee you smelled wasn't mine. It was his."

Griselda shook her head sadly.

"When people see that video, they'll think I'm a *puta*."

"They won't think that at all. They'll know you're a victim."

"Maybe some of them will know I'm a victim, but most of them will think I'm a *puta*. I mean, who else would let all those guys have sex with her."

"You didn't let them do it."

"I know I didn't. But at times I feel like I did. I don't know where that feeling comes from, but I can't help it."

"Then just keep telling yourself you didn't let them do it."

"Okay. I didn't let them do it."

Griselda got up and came to her and hugged her, saying: "I'll pray to Our Lady of Altagracia. I'll ask her to stop you from feeling like you let them do it. And I'll ask her to stop you from being pregnant."

"*Gracias*," Esperanza said, returning the hug.

On her way home she stopped at the drugstore on Palisade Avenue and bought two pregnancy tests. The same guy was behind the counter, and he looked at her knowingly. Unlike the pill, she couldn't take the test while walking to the bus stop. She had to wait until she got home, where she went directly to the bathroom, wishing there was a lock on the door. At least her family had a convention that if the door was closed, the bathroom was occupied.

She had decided to use one of the tests right away though she still had five or six days before her period was due. If she was pregnant, she wanted to know as soon as possible. From the directions that came with the test she understood that it could detect the presence of some hormone in her urine, and that the level of this hormone might not yet be high enough to be detected, which would give her a false negative. But if it was already high enough, the test would be positive, and she would know if she was pregnant.

When the test came out negative she wasn't relieved since she knew it could still be positive, and she hid the remaining test in a drawer under the sweaters she wouldn't need until it got colder. She was glad her father was working that night since in her predicament it was harder to face him than her mother. Thinking of her father, she leaned toward the option of killing herself if the test came out positive.

The next day she had classes in English and history. The English course met twice a week, but the history course met only once a week, so it was a long class, and after being subjected to a lecture for most of it, she was numb with fatigue. She wandered to the cafeteria and went out the door that led to a patio which overlooked the athletic fields. Soccer was the big sport in the fall, but the guys on the field now weren't playing soccer. They were running around with long sticks that had pouches at their ends. She knew they were members of the lacrosse team, practicing and getting into shape for the spring. They were mostly big guys, and running around with those sticks, they frightened her.

She was standing at the edge of the patio when she became aware of someone behind her. She turned and saw it was the guy who had tried to stop her in the hall, and she braced herself for an encounter that she believed could only make things worse.

The guy was holding out his hand to her, and in his hand was her silver locket.

"Please take it," he begged her.

She wanted to take the locket, but she was held back by a series of thoughts that raced through her mind. Again, she recognized his voice, and she was certain that he was the guy who had pinned her arms. His having the locket seemed to confirmed this. So if she took it, he would be relieved of the evidence against him. Also, he would know for sure that she was the girl they had raped together. So she refused to take it, saying: "It doesn't belong to me."

"Yeah, it does. I know it does."

"You don't know anything. Leave me alone."

"I'm not going to hurt you. I only want to return something that I know you value."

"You don't know what I value," she told him. "You don't know anything about me."

He dangled the locket in front of her, saying: "Please take it."

"I told you, it doesn't belong to me."

"I know it belongs to you. I saw you wearing it."

"You're confusing me with another girl," she said, turning away from him. "And don't follow me. If you do, I'll call security. I'll say you're stalking me."

She walked toward the door of the cafeteria in a mire of feelings. Surprisingly, there was pity for him mixed with her anger against him. But her anger prevailed. And as much as it hurt her not to have the locket, she firmly believed that she had done the right thing. From his pleas she could tell he felt remorse for what he had done, and that having the locket reminded him of it. Believing that the only way he could get rid of the locket was by returning it to her, she resolved not to accept it from him.

FIVE

JEFFREY STOOD ON the patio, watching the girl walk away. He was stunned by her refusal to take the locket. He didn't understand her behavior. He could tell from the look of recognition in her dark eyes that the locket did belong to her, and that it was something of value to her. So why had she told him it didn't belong to her? Why had she refused to take it?

Maybe she sensed his need to return it. Maybe she understood that for him, returning the locket was the necessary first step toward reconciliation. And maybe she wanted him to suffer for a while longer. But maybe she would never take the locket. Maybe she would deny him a chance to relieve himself of the guilt he felt for what he had done to her. As usual when he remembered it, he felt as if he had pinned the arms of Jesus while they drove the nails into his hands, and he groaned in despair at the prospect of always having to live with this feeling.

He had to talk with Father Paul, so he left the campus and walked to St. Brigid, where he found the priest outside the front door, smoking a cigarette. He thought he had smelled cigarette smoke the first time he went to see Father Paul, but he hadn't wanted to believe it. He had never seen a priest smoking.

"You're back," Father Paul said, snuffing out the cigarette and dropping it into a receptacle that must have been there for the use of parishioners.

"Yeah," Jeffrey said. "I need to talk with you."

"Okay, come in." Father Paul opened the door for him and followed him in.

They sat in the pew where they had sat before.

"I found the girl, and I tried to return the locket to her, as you advised me. But she wouldn't take it. She said it didn't belong to her."

"Are you sure it was the right girl?"

"Yeah, I'm sure. I'll never forget her face."

The priest frowned. "I wonder why she wouldn't take it."

"Maybe she didn't want to relieve me of my guilt."

"That's possible. It's also possible that she didn't want to relieve you of the evidence."

"I didn't think of that," Jeffrey said. "I'm not worried about her bringing charges against me."

"Because she can't identify you?"

"I think she *can* identify me. I think she recognized my voice."

"And you had the locket to remind her. So why aren't you worried about her bringing charges against you?"

"Well, I don't think she wants to appear in court."

"I don't think so either. It would be a humiliating experience for her."

"But something could make her feel she has nothing to lose by bringing charges against us."

The priest waited for him to explain.

"They made a video of what we did to her."

"They did? Oh, no." Father Paul closed his eyes as if he was saying a prayer for the girl.

"Their leader wants to post the video on a website."

"There are websites that show such videos?"

"Oh, yeah. There are sites that specialize in gang rapes."

"Lord, forgive us," Father Paul murmured. "How far we've strayed from your love and grace."

"I tried to convince him not to post the video, but I don't know if I succeeded."

"What did you tell him?"

"Since he has no morals, I told him it would put him at risk of being caught. But he said there wasn't any risk because the video doesn't show our faces."

"Does it have your voices?"

"I don't think it does."

"You mean you didn't watch it?"

"I wouldn't *ever* watch that video," Jeffrey said. "It's bad enough remembering what we did to her."

Father Paul reflected. "So you think that if they post the video on a website, where everyone in the world can watch it, she'll feel she has nothing to lose by bringing charges against you?"

"Yeah, that's what I think."

"Then if I were you, I'd try again to stop them from posting that video."

"I'll try again. But I only want to stop it for her sake. I don't care if it puts us at risk of being caught. I almost wish we *would* be caught."

"I understand. You feel you should atone for what you did. And frankly, you should—but not by going to prison."

"How should I atone for it?"

"To start with, by repenting and asking for forgiveness."

"You mean asking God for forgiveness?"

"Yes. But that'll be the easy part. If you're truly sorry for what you did, then God will forgive you. The hard part will be asking the girl for forgiveness."

"So I have to do more than return her locket."

"Returning her locket is only the first step in a long process."

"But what if she won't let me take the first step?"

"I believe she will, eventually," Father Paul told him. "You have to keep trying. And for her sake you have to keep trying to stop them from posting that video."

Back in his room he found Kenny lying on his bed, playing on his smartphone. Without looking up, Kenny asked: "Why weren't you at practice today?"

"I had a doctor's appointment," he said.

"The coach wasn't happy. You better have a note from the doctor."

"You mean he won't believe me without a note?"

"I'm your roommate, and I don't believe you, so why would the coach believe you?"

Not wanting to be dragged farther into a conversation that would lead nowhere, Jeffrey changed the subject. "You know that video of what we did?"

"Yeah, what about it?"

"You shouldn't post it on a website."

"We already did."

"What?" His stomach heaved.

"Here, you can watch it," Kenny told him, finding it on his smartphone.

"I don't want to watch it. I want you to take it down."

"Well, you'll have to talk with Brandon about it. He was the one who posted it. But I don't think you can take something down once you've posted it."

"There must be a way to take it down."

"I'll text him now. I think he's in his room."

A few minutes later Brandon and Scott came into the room, occupying what little remained of its compact space.

"What's the problem?" Brandon asked, leaning against the door as if he wanted to prevent anyone from leaving.

"Kenny said you posted that video."

"Yeah, I did. And I've gotten thousands of hits on it. I wish I could monetize it."

"If you posted it on YouTube," Scott suggested, "you could monetize it."

"YouTube would never allow that kind of content."

"I want you to take the video down," Jeffrey told Brandon.

"You do? Why? Are you dating that spic?"

"You can't imagine how that girl will feel if everyone can watch her being raped?"

"We didn't rape her," Scott insisted. "We only gave her what she wanted."

"Even if we did rape her," Brandon said, "is there any reason why we shouldn't let everyone watch that video?"

"Yeah. It will humiliate her."

"How do you know? How do you know she hasn't told her friends about it? For a girl like that it's a big deal having sex with four lacrosse players."

"Three lacrosse players," Scott pointed out. "Jeffrey didn't take his turn."

"He pinned her arms. Without Jeffrey we couldn't have done it."

Kenny patted him on the shoulder, saying: "Yeah, you were a valuable member of the team."

Ignoring him, Jeffrey said: "If you don't take it down, I'll go to the disciplinary committee and tell them what we did."

There was a sudden silence.

Then Brandon laughed. "You have a good sense of humor."

"I'm not kidding. If you don't take that video down, I'll go to the disciplinary committee."

"If you do that," Scott said, "we'll get expelled."

"I don't care if I get expelled. In fact, I don't care if I go to prison. I deserve to be expelled, and I deserve to go to prison."

"Maybe you do," Brandon told him, "but we don't. So you're not going to the disciplinary committee."

"You can't stop me."

"Yeah, I can. I can give you a taste of what'll happen if you go to that committee."

Jeffrey braced himself, standing his ground while Brandon picked up his lacrosse stick.

"Hold his arms," Brandon ordered the other two guys.

Though he struggled fiercely, Jeffrey couldn't fight them off. They turned him around and got each arm in a painful hammerlock.

Brandon reached around and unbuckled his belt and took down his pants. And then with the lacrosse stick he started whacking his bare ass and the backs of his thighs.

It hurt like hell, but Jeffrey didn't let out a cry. He gritted his teeth and bore the pain, feeling he deserved it. The harder Brandon whacked him, the closer he felt to that poor girl, and it helped him to imagine how she had suffered.

After breaking the stick Brandon finally stopped, and the other two guys let go of his arms.

Jeffrey pulled up his pants and buckled his belt and faced them.

"Well, that's just a taste of what'll happen if you go to that committee," Brandon told him.

"Your father will have to buy you a new stick," Scott said, holding one of its pieces.

"I don't need a lacrosse stick," Jeffrey said.

"Are you going to play without one?" Kenny sniped.

"I'm quitting the team."

"If you do, you'll lose your scholarship."

"I don't need a scholarship."

"Are you dropping out of college?"

"No. I'm going to take loans like other people do."

"Well, I don't care what you do," Brandon said, "as long as you don't go to the disciplinary committee."

Jeffrey said nothing. He went to the door and opened it.

"Where are you going?" Brandon demanded as if he had a right to know.

"I'm going to request a single room. And until I get one, I'm going to stay at a motel." With that he left and closed the door behind him.

He went to the office of residential life and filed a request for a single room. The girl said he could have one within a few days since a guy with a single had just dropped out. She took his phone number and said she would call him as soon as the room was available.

Then he went to the office of financial aid and met with a girl who checked his account. She explained that when the college gave athletic scholarships it always used whatever grants were available from the federal and state governments, and since his parents didn't have a high level of income, some money from grants had been credited to his account. But he hadn't taken any loans, so the full amount was still available.

He thanked her and told her he would return after talking with his parents. And finally he went to talk with the coach, whom he found in an office near the gym.

The coach looked up from a paper on his desk and said: "You missed practice today."

"I'm sorry," he said, realizing that he didn't have to lie about having a doctor's appointment. Instead, he told the truth: "I'm quitting the team."

"You're what?" the coach said in disbelief.

"I'm quitting the team," he repeated.

"You can't quit the team. We need you, Jeffrey. You're one of our top players."

"Thanks. But I can't play a sport and do well in my courses. I thought I could, but I'm falling behind, and I don't want to flunk out of college."

"You won't flunk out of college. I just got a report from one of your professors," the coach said, looking through the papers on his desk. "It says you're doing well. It says you're one of the top students in the course."

"Well, I'm not doing well in my other courses."

The coach examined him, asking: "Is there something wrong?"

"No, there's nothing wrong."

"Are you sure?"

"I'm sure."

"Well, if there is, you should tell me."

"If there was, I would."

The coach sighed. "I can't stop you. But if you change your mind, I want you to know you'll always have a place on my team."

"Thanks," he said.

"Good luck," the coach said, shaking his hand.

The next step was to call his father and tell him he had quit lacrosse. For some reason it was easier to lie to his father than to his mother, and he planned to tell his father the same lie he had told the coach. He knew his father would be at the restaurant at this hour, getting things ready for dinner, which started with senior citizens around five.

He walked to the other side of the tennis courts, where there wouldn't be any foot traffic, and he punched the number of his father's phone.

"It's me," he said when his father answered.

"Hey, Jeffrey. How are you doing?" his father asked him as if he assumed that everything was fine.

"I'm doing okay. I just called to let you know I quit lacrosse."

"You did? Why?"

"I can't play a sport and do well in my courses."

"I thought you were doing well in your courses. Are they getting harder?" Since his father hadn't gone to college, he could only guess what the problem might be.

"No, but I've begun to fall behind. I've also discovered," he added, wanting to include an element of truth in his pack of lies, "that I don't have anything in common with some members of the team."

"You're rooming with a member of the team, aren't you?"

"I was, but I've requested a change."

"You weren't getting along?"

"We were getting along, but I couldn't study with him in the room. He was always playing games on his smartphone."

"Okay. It's your decision," his father said. "But if you quit lacrosse, will you lose your scholarship?"

"I will, but I can take loans like most of the other students do."

"Well, I don't want you to graduate from college with a load of debt."

"I won't. The tuition here is lower than at other private colleges. And if I do really well in my courses, I might get an academic scholarship."

"That would be great. And I can help with the tuition. The restaurant's having a good year."

Jeffrey knew from having worked at the restaurant that it needed a good February and a good August to have a good year, and both months had been good. "Thanks. I'll let you know when I have to replace the scholarship."

After saying goodbye he felt he had gotten off easy. But he knew it would be a lot harder when he told both his parents the truth.

He wasn't surprised to learn that the head of the disciplinary committee was the nun who taught his business ethics course. Since he couldn't imagine going to her and admitting what he had done to that girl, he delayed taking action and sought advice from Father Paul, whom he found again in front of the church smoking a cigarette.

"I know," Father Paul said as if he had noticed a look of disapproval, "it's bad for my health. But I've been smoking since I was younger than you."

"Did you start smoking in Ireland?"

"I did. So I was glad when they transferred me to this country because it has better cigarettes."

"How long have you been in this country?"

"Let's see. I came here in the summer of 1993, so that makes it twenty-three years."

"You've been in this country longer than I've been alive."

Father Paul nodded. "I guess I have. So I should know as much about this country as you do, shouldn't I."

"I'm sure you know more."

When the priest had snuffed out his cigarette and dropped it into the receptacle they went into the church and took their usual seats.

"I tried again to stop them from posting the video," Jeffrey said. "But it was too late. They'd already posted it."

"Did you try to get them to take it down?"

"I did, but they wouldn't. So I said that if they didn't take it down, I'd go to the disciplinary committee and tell them what we did to that girl."

"I'll bet they didn't like that."

"They didn't," Jeffrey said. "And to give me a taste of what they'd do to me if I went to that committee, they held my arms and whacked me with my lacrosse stick."

"Ouch. Did they do any serious damage to you?"

"I only have some welts and bruises."

"What about the girl? Does she know they've posted a video of it?"

"If she doesn't already, she'll know soon. The guy who posted it said it had gotten thousands of hits. So everyone on campus will know about it."

"Then going back to your reasoning," Father Paul said after a pause, "she'll be so humiliated she'll feel she has nothing to lose by charging you guys with rape."

"Well, after what they did to me, I have a better understanding of what we did to her. I mean, what we did was much worse, but it gave me an inkling."

"That's progress. So what are you going to do with your better understanding?"

"I'm going to go to the disciplinary committee and tell them everything."

"Did you come to ask me if I think that's a good idea?"

"I actually came to ask you if you know the nun who's head of the disciplinary committee."

"What's her name?"

"Sister Maura."

The eyes of the priest lit up. "Of course I know her. We go way back, though she goes back farther than I do. I could tell you lot about her, but I think you want to know if she's the kind of person who would listen to you and not judge you."

"Yeah, that's what I want to know."

"Well, she *is* that kind of person. I'd even go as far as saying you're lucky she's head of that committee."

"Then I'll talk with her, and I'll tell her everything."

Father Paul made a steeple of his hands and said: "Now, that'll set the wheels of justice in motion, but it won't get you any closer to a reconciliation."

"If the girl won't take the locket, then I can't get anywhere with her."

"If you gave it to Sister Maura, then she'd still be able to testify that you had the locket in your possession, so there wouldn't be a problem of your getting rid of the evidence."

"I tried to give it to Sister Maura, but she wouldn't take it."

With a faint smile Father Paul said: "It sounds like no one will take the locket from you. Did Sister Maura tell you why she wouldn't take it?"

"I told her you'd advised me to return the locket to the girl, and she said that if she returned it for me, I might not have another chance for a reconciliation."

"She's a wise person. She understood what I was trying to do. But the situation has changed because of that video. So your tactics have to change."

He waited for the priest to elaborate.

"I'll talk with Sister Maura, and I'll explain why I think you should give her the locket so that she can return it to the girl."

"You think she'll agree to return it for me?"

"Well, I don't have any power over her, but I do have some influence. So let's see."

He waited until the next day, giving Father Paul time to contact Sister Maura, and then he went to her office in Farrell Hall. He knew when her office hours were, and he hoped he wouldn't find other students waiting to see her.

There weren't any students in the waiting area, and evidently there wasn't a student in her office since the receptionist told him to go right in.

"Please sit down," she said kindly. "Father Paul called me yesterday, and he explained the situation."

"So you know what we did to that girl?"

"Yes. I know what you did to her."

"Oh, God," he cried. "How can I ever atone for it ?"

"Well, you can start by giving me the locket."

"If I give it to you, will you give it to her?"

"Of course I will. But before I take it from you," Sister Maura said, "I want you to acknowledge that you had the locket in your possession, and that you wanted her to have it."

"You do? Why?"

"So I can reassure her that you're not trying to get rid of the evidence."

"But that's not why I want to return it."

"I know it's not. But other people might not understand why you wanted to return it."

"All right," he said after thinking about it. "I'll do whatever you say."

She pushed a pad and a pen toward him, saying: "I want you to write, in your own words, a statement of why you want to return the locket."

He sat there as if she had given him an exam.

"It'll help you understand your feelings."

He picked up the pen and hesitated, not knowing where to begin.

"You don't have to write the whole story. You only have to write why you want to return the locket to her."

"I want to return the locket to—" he wrote, and then he realized that after all that had happened he didn't know her name. "What's her name?"

"Her name is Esperanza. It means 'hope' in Spanish."

"How do you spell it?"

Sister Maura spelled it for him.

"—Esperanza," he wrote, "because it's something of value to her, and because it's the only thing of value that I can return."

"Is that it?" the nun asked when he had stopped.

"No, there's more." He continued writing. "I hope that if she takes it, then someday she'll forgive me."

"Is that it?"

"Yeah, that's it."

"Please read it to me."

As he read his statement to Sister Maura he found that it *had* helped him understand his feelings. It had helped him understand how much he wanted Esperanza to forgive him. He believed that God would forgive him, but he didn't believe that she would forgive him. He could only hope that someday she would.

"That's good," Sister Maura said. "Now, sign your name to it."

"This isn't a confession, is it?"

"A confession is something you make to a priest, and I'm not a priest, as you pointed out the first time we met."

"I meant a confession that can be used in court."

"You have my word that it won't be used for that purpose. It will only be used to reassure Esperanza."

He realized that knowing her name had changed her from a collective girl to an individual person, which made him feel even worse.

Sister Maura waited patiently.

He signed the paper and handed it to her.

"Thank you," she said. "Now, let's see the locket."

He dug into the pocket of his jeans and took out the envelope into which he had put the locket. He opened the envelope and shook the locket with its chain onto the desk.

Sister Maura picked up the locket and opened it, saying: "Our Lady of Guadalupe."

"When will you return it?"

"As soon as I can, but it's not easy for faculty to contact students. They don't respond to our emails, and we don't have their cell phone numbers, so we can't send them text messages. But I'll see her on Thursday in my freshman seminar, and I can return it then."

"Okay." He cleared his throat and broached the next subject. "I heard that you're head of the disciplinary committee."

"I'm head by default since no one else wants that position."

"Well, I want to go to the committee and tell them what we did to Esperanza."

Looking surprised, Sister Maura said: "You do? Why?"

"I feel we shouldn't get away with it."

"I understand. But have you thought about how *she* would feel having to tell the committee what you did to her?"

"It's already pubic knowledge. They made a video, which they posted on a website."

"I know," Sister Maura sighed.

"How did you know?"

"Father Paul told me. He told me you tried to stop them from posting it, and then you tried to get them to take it down."

"I tried, but I didn't get anywhere."

"Does it show her face?"

"I haven't seen it, but they say it does. I think they wanted to show her face."

"You mean they wanted to humiliate her publicly?"

"Yeah. I think they have something against girls. From the way they talk about girls, I think they consider them as objects, not as humans."

Sister Maura shook her head sadly. "We see that everywhere in the world, but I never thought we'd see it here at this college."

"This was originally a college for women, wasn't it?"

"It was. And most of the sisters were dead set against opening enrollment to men."

"So anyway," Jeffrey resumed, "I want to go to the disciplinary committee and tell them what we did to Esperanza."

"I understand how that would help you," Sister Maura said. "But how would it help *her?*"

"I don't know. I guess it would help her get justice."

"But what if she doesn't need justice? What if she needs something else?"

"What do you mean?"

"I mean mercy."

"Well, I don't see how I could help her get mercy. Though I do see," he added, "how I could have helped her get mercy when I realized what they were going to do to her."

"I'm glad you see that," Sister Maura said. "And I hope you see how taking the matter to the disciplinary committee could hurt Esperanza."

"I know it would be hard for her. But I think it would be even harder for her if everyone sees that video and draws the wrong conclusions from it."

"That's a good point. But it's not your decision to take the matter to the disciplinary committee. The normal process is for the victim to take the matter to the committee, and unless she does, we can't do anything."

"I thought that if I brought it to your attention, you could do something."

"Believe me, I want to do something. I don't want students at this college who do such barbarous things. In fact, I don't want them at any college. But before we can proceed with a hearing, the victim has to file a complaint."

"You can't act on her behalf?"

"If it was another kind of matter, I could. But in this kind of matter there are policies and procedures that we have to follow."

"So there's nothing you can do?"

"There's one thing I can do," Sister Maura said. "When I return the locket to her, I can talk with her about taking the matter to the committee. She can't spend her whole life hiding what happened to her. Sooner or later, she'll have to come out with it."

"Whenever she's ready, I'll support her."

Sister Maura looked as if she had gotten an idea. "If she decides to tell her parents what happened to her, will you go with her and support her story?"

"Yeah, I will," he said without having to think about it.

"Good. I'll let her know that."

He left Sister Maura's office feeling that his life was in the hands of Esperanza, and he hoped she would decide to take the matter to the committee. But he understood why she wouldn't want to tell her parents about it. He still hadn't mustered the courage to tell his own parents about it.

SIX

AFTER A DINNER of mixed greens salad with grilled chicken Maura went into the chapel that was attached to the convent. It was in the modern style, in a hexagon with the altar in the center. It was designed by a famous architect who had done the project pro bono as a donation to the sisters. It wasn't the kind of religious space that Maura had grown up with, but over the years she had gotten used to it.

She sat down at the end of a pew, aware of being the only person in the chapel. Later, some of her colleagues would arrive for evening prayer, and in the morning they would all be there for the six o'clock mass, even the ones who got around by wheelchair. There were less than fifty of them now, compared with more than two hundred of them in the middle of the last century. That had been the peak, and during the Seventies and the Eighties their numbers had declined through resignations, deaths, and the lack of new recruits. Maura believed that the two main reasons for this decline were the limits imposed on the role of women in the church and the choices opened to women in the labor market. She had to admit that if she were a girl of eighteen now, she might have chosen another profession.

But she had few regrets. She loved teaching, and she had a feeling of accomplishment for all the other things she had done to build the college. So she prayed for Esperanza, she prayed for Jeffrey, and she prayed for the college, whose reputation could be damaged by what those guys had done. She was also supposed to pray for those guys, but she couldn't make herself pray for them. She found herself wanting to talk with Paul about it, not because he was a priest but because he was a man and might have insights into male behavior that were beyond her. Of course he could have been her son, but they had developed a peer relationship over the years since he was assigned to celebrate the daily mass at the college, replacing Justin who had suddenly died of a heart attack. At the time Paul was in his early twenties, fresh from Ireland with a thick brogue. He was based at St. Brigid, the nearest church, and he lived there with its pastor in the rectory. From there he was sent to St. Ann, where he served as assistant pastor for several years, and then he was brought back to St. Brigid, where he served as pastor. His brogue was thinner now, but he still smoked as much as before, though he had tried a number of times to give up smoking.

She would see him in the chapel the next morning at the six o'clock mass, but they wouldn't have enough time to talk since he had to get back to St. Brigid for the eight o'clock and she had an eight-thirty class, and they would both be busy for the rest of the day, so she decided to meet him that evening. After making a final petition to the Blessed Mother, she left the chapel and headed down the hall with her phone already in her hand. While still moving, she punched his number and waited for his phone to ring.

"Father Paul," he said, answering.

"Hi, it's Maura."

"Well, what do you know? We were just talking about you today."

"You and one of our students?"

"Yeah. How did you guess?"

"I know everything," she joked. "Are you free tonight?"

"I'm as free as I get. Do you have anything particular in mind?"

"I'd like to talk with you about this situation."

"Sure. Should I come to the college?"

"No, let's meet at that bar on Palisade."

"What bar?" he asked as if he didn't know there was a bar on Palisade.

"The last time I went there it was called Hogan's."

"It's still called Hogan's."

"So let's meet there in twenty minutes. Okay?"

"Okay. I'll see you at Hogan's."

The bar was a ten-minute walk from the college. It had been one of the local bars where she and Audrey went for relaxation, away from the college. They had their best conversations in bars, and Maura missed talking with her friend, who had died of cancer seven years ago. They had been through a lot together, dealing with one crisis after another. At least Audrey had lived to see them overcome the last crisis, when they stopped the chairman of the board of trustees from selling the college's property to a developer. In his eyes they were sitting on a hundred acres of prime real estate that overlooked the Hudson River, doing nothing with it to make money. Solana had joined them in that fight, contributing her youth, her energy, and her unwavering commitment to the college's mission.

As usual the bar was filled with guys in work clothes. The only change was that with the ban on smoking in public places there was no longer smoke in the air.

She spotted Paul sitting in a booth with a glass of Guinness in front of him, and she joined him, conscious of being the only woman in the place. When she had come here with Audrey she had been in her element, but without Audrey it was different.

Being a well-raised Irish boy, Paul got up and greeted her with a social hug and asked her what she was drinking.

"I'll have a white wine, the house wine."

"That's the only kind of wine they have," he said, smiling. "This is a beer place."

He went to the bar and got a glass of wine and returned to the booth with it.

"So," he said after sitting down. "Did he give you the locket?"

She nodded. "Yeah. And now I have to give it to her."

"You sound like you have doubts."

"I don't have doubts. But I do have feelings I've never had before."

"You mean about what those guys did?"

"Yeah. I know guys do that kind of thing. I read in the paper every day about guys raping women, torturing women, and killing women. But I never expected it to happen on our campus."

"It could happen anywhere."

"It could, but I like to think of our campus as a sanctuary where students don't have to worry about the kind of things that happen in their neighborhoods."

"I understand. They violated your vision of the college."

"That's how I feel. And in some way I feel responsible for what they did."

"I wouldn't go that far. You couldn't stop it from happening."

"No, but I can stop it from happening again."

"By having those guys expelled?"

"It'll get them off the campus, and it'll send a clear message that we're not going to tolerate violence against women."

"You want to do that through the disciplinary committee?"

"I want to, but I can't do anything unless the girl brings charges against those guys. And I understand why she doesn't want to appear before the committee."

Paul nodded. "Yeah, that would be humiliating."

"It would, but more importantly she doesn't want her parents to know about it."

"How could her parents not know about it?"

"Well, I'm sure they don't watch videos of gang rapes."

"But someone who does watch videos of gang rapes could tell them what happened to their daughter."

Maura sighed. "I can't imagine anyone telling them about it. But then I can't imagine raping a girl and making a video of it."

"And then posting it on a website."

"You're a male. Can you explain why they would want to hurt that girl?"

"They must hate women."

"Why do they hate women? Do they blame their mothers for not loving them enough?"

"I don't know if they blame their mothers, but they must blame women for their problems. It's easy to blame other people for your problems."

"So what they did to Esperanza was a hate crime?"

"I think it was," Paul said. "But I don't understand why Jeffrey went along with them. He seems like a good boy."

"He does, and that's what frightens me. I mean, if boys like him are doing that kind of thing to girls, what hope can we have for society?"

"It doesn't help that they're bombarded with scenes of violence from all directions."

"It doesn't help," Maura agreed, having gotten glimpses of what her students viewed on their smartphones. "I know there are studies which conclude that playing violent games or watching violent movies doesn't make people more likely to commit acts of violence, but I don't believe them. Those games and those movies teach people to regard humans as objects."

"Then we should blame the games and the movies?"

"No, people can still choose how they act in the real world. And though I feel sympathy for Jeffrey, he chose to go along with those guys."

"At least he's sorry for what he did."

"He *is* sorry for what he did, but that's not enough. He has to do something about it."

"I agree. It's not enough for him just to have feelings."

"I was hoping he could start the process of reconciliation by returning the locket, but that didn't work."

"Well, you could start the process for him."

"That's what I intend to do. And I do believe there's hope for a reconciliation."

"You sound like you feel it's your job to make it happen."

"I feel it's my job to help them. But if they don't want it to happen, I can't make it happen. I've learned that much after fifty years of being a teacher."

Paul smiled. "I still haven't learned that after twenty-three years of being a priest."

"Are you learning anything from your assistant?"

"You mean my temporary assistant."

They were referring to the priest from Ghana who had been assigned to St. Brigid while pursuing his studies at Dunwoodie. He had celebrated mass for the sisters a few days ago, and some of them had complained about not being able to understand him.

"How long will you have him?"

"Through next summer."

"And then what?"

"I don't know. There aren't enough priests in the pipeline."

"Well, you know what I think. If they allowed priests to marry, then we wouldn't have a shortage of them."

"That seems to work for the Protestants."

"They also allow women to be priests. So if those old men in Rome, who are still living back in the Middle Ages, allowed those changes, we wouldn't have a problem."

"I'll suggest that to the pope."

"I like him," Maura said. "He's the first pope I've liked in fifty years. So maybe we'll finally have some changes."

"Maybe we will," Paul said after emptying his glass of Guinness. "But meanwhile we have to promote a reconciliation."

Back in her room, Maura picked up the locket from her night table, where she had left it. A link in the chain was broken, indicating that the locket had been ripped from the girl's neck. To avoid tampering with evidence, she had previously decided not to fix it, but since she had promised not to use the locket as evidence, she changed her mind.

She had a colleague, Eleanor, whose father had been a jeweler, and she had inherited his tools, which she used to replace batteries of watches and to repair chains. So after mass the next morning Maura went to Eleanor's room and showed her the locket. Eleanor examined the chain for a moment and said she could fix it. In fact, it would take her only a few seconds, so Maura waited while Eleanor used a pair of fine needle-nose pliers to fix the chain.

For some reason she was afraid that Esperanza would cut the class, and she was relieved to see the girl at her usual desk in the center of the room. She was hoping to have an extended conversation with her, so when the class ended, she discreetly approached the girl and asked: "Are you free now?"

"Yeah, why?" Esperanza asked suspiciously.

"I have something for you," Maura said, "and I'd like you to come with me to my office so I can give it to you."

"Why can't you give it to me here?"

"I want to talk with you, and we don't have any privacy here."

"Well, what do you want to talk with me about?"

"I'll tell you in my office." She restrained the impulse to put her arm around the girl and guide her away since under the current set of rules, which had been established in response to the fear of pedophilia, you weren't allowed to touch students for any reason.

Surprisingly, the girl came along with her without any further encouragement.

"I hope I'm not failing your course," Esperanza said as if that might be the reason why the professor wanted to talk with her.

"No, you're not failing. You're doing fine."

"I know I missed a class."

"It's all right. I gave you an excused absence."

"Thanks," the girl said gratefully.

As they walked across the campus Maura asked: "Do you live in Yonkers?"

"Yeah. I live with my family in an apartment on South Broadway."

"Do you have any brothers or sisters?"

"I have one brother."

"How old is he?"

"He's fifteen."

"Where are your parents from?"

"Mexico. They're U.S. citizens now, and I am too because I was born here."

"What does your father do for a living?"

"He's a cook at an Italian restaurant. He's the number two guy in the kitchen," Esperanza said proudly.

"What about your mother?"

"She's a nursing assistant at St. Joseph's Hospital."

"Do you have a job?"

"I work at a Dominican restaurant on Fridays, Saturdays, and Sundays."

"Have you decided on a career?"

"I want to be a physician's assistant."

She was a typical St. Catherine student: she lived in Yonkers, her parents were immigrants, she worked three days a week while going to college, and she wanted a career in service. In fact, she was the purpose of Maura's vocation.

By now they had reached Farrell Hall, and Maura opened the front door and let Esperanza into the building ahead of her.

"It's this way," she said, heading toward her office.

She unlocked the door, and after they had entered her office she closed it behind them, letting people know she didn't want any interruptions.

"Please sit down," she told the girl, gesturing toward the chair beside her desk.

Esperanza very carefully lowered herself as if there might be something on the chair that she would crush.

After settling in the chair behind her desk, Maura opened her pocketbook and took out the locket and dangled it by the chain in the space between her and the girl. "Is this yours?

Esperanza only stared at the locket.

"Take it and see if it's yours," Maura said.

The girl hesitated but finally reached out and took the locket. She opened it and gazed at the picture inside it, saying: "Yeah, it's mine. How did you get it?"

"The boy who tried to give it to you gave it to me, so that I could give it to you. He wants you to have it."

"Why does he want me to have it?" Esperanza asked with tears forming in her dark eyes.

"I believe he understands that it's something of value to you."

"It's not possible." By now the tears were streaming down her cheeks. "It's not possible after what he did to me."

"What did he do to you?" Maura asked gently.

"He ruined my life," Esperanza cried. "I mean, the four of them ruined my life."

"I know what they did, so you can talk with me about it."

"You know?" The girl looked at her as if she couldn't believe that a nun would know about such things. And she cried: "Oh, God. If *you* know, then everyone knows."

"I don't think everyone knows. Your parents still don't know, do they?"

"No. But if they find out about it, I might as well kill myself."

"You think they wouldn't understand?"

"I know they wouldn't," Esperanza said with certainty. "How could my parents ever understand why I let those guys have sex with me?"

"You didn't let those guys have sex with you," Maura told her. "They raped you."

"My father won't see it that way. He'll think I let them, and in his eyes I'll be a *puta*."

"You think that if you explain what happened, he won't believe you?"

"Why should he believe me?"

"You're his daughter. He loves you."

"He loves me now, but if he finds out about it," Esperanza said with a torrent of tears, "he won't love me anymore."

After reflecting, Maura said: "I'm afraid that sooner or later your parents *will* find out about it. Those guys made a video of it, which they posted on a website, and someone who knows your family might see the video and recognize you and tell your parents. Sooner or later, that's bound to happen."

"I know," the girl murmured.

"I think it would be better if your parents learn about it from you than from someone else. At least then you'll have a chance to explain what happened before they make any judgment about it."

"My father still wouldn't believe me."

"What would it take for him to believe you?"

"I don't know. If I killed myself, he might believe me."

"If you killed yourself," Maura said, "he might believe you did it because you couldn't bear to live with your sin. So don't even think about killing yourself."

Esperanza stared bleakly at the picture in the locket. "You're a nun. Can you explain why God let those guys rape me?"

"I can't explain why. And even if I could, I think it's too soon for you to understand why it happened."

"You think eventually I will understand?"

"I think you will."

"But if there *is* no explanation, then I'll never understand why it happened."

To prevent the girl from going down that road, Maura said: "Well, let's go back to our immediate concern. We were wondering what it would take for your father to believe you, and we ruled out killing yourself. Do you have any other ideas?"

Esperanza shook her head, saying: "I don't know what it would take for him to believe me. No matter what I told him, he wouldn't believe me."

"I understand. Then maybe you'll have to *do* something to make him believe you."

"Like what?"

"I don't know," Maura said, trying to think of something.

After a silence Esperanza said: "I don't understand why that guy wanted to return my locket. Is he hoping I'll forgive him?"

"I believe he is."

"Did he tell you about it?"

"He told me enough about it. He told a priest more about it, and the priest asked me to take the locket from that guy and give it to you."

"What's his name?"

"His name is Jeffrey."

Esperanza nodded as if she might have guessed such a name, and then she said: "You know, he didn't rape me."

"What *did* he do?"

"He pinned my arms with his knees and clamped his hands around my wrists." She pulled up a sleeve of her shirt, saying: "See the bruises?"

There were purple splotches on her upper arm.

"So he's not innocent," Esperanza said.

"He's certainly not innocent. But he *is* sorry for what he did."

"Then God will forgive him?"

"God will forgive us anything if we're sorry for it."

"Well, I don't see how I can forgive him."

"It's too soon. But I can see how he might help you with your father," Maura said, thinking of the bruises.

"How?" the girl asked skeptically.

"If he went with you when you told your father what happened to you, he could support your story. You could show your father the bruises on your arms, and Jeffrey could tell your father how he pinned you."

Esperanza considered. "Yeah, he could. But my father might still think I let them do it."

"After seeing the bruises?"

"Yeah, he might think we had rough sex."

"He won't think that, not after seeing how sorry Jeffrey is."

"It might work. But I can't ask him to help me."

"I know you can't ask him," Maura said. "But I can ask him, or the priest can ask him."

Esperanza closed the locket as if she was ending the conversation. "Thanks for giving this back to me. At least I don't have to keep lying about it."

"You mean about the locket."

"Yeah, though I still have to keep lying about what happened." The girl appealed to Maura with despair in her eyes. "I'm lying to them by not telling them about it. And I feel guilty about lying to them. But I don't want to relieve my guilt by telling them the truth since I know how much it would hurt them. I mean, it would break my father's heart."

"I understand. It's not a bad reason for lying to them. But while you're lying to them, you're depriving yourself of the comfort they could give you."

"I don't see what comfort they could give me."

"You'll see," Maura said, "when they give it to you. Trust me."

Esperanza pulled the ends of the chain behind her neck and without much trouble fastened the clasp. She straightened the locket, which hung out over the front of her shirt, and she got up, saying: "Thanks again. And let me think about your idea."

"Before you go, I'll give you something else to think about. The college has a professional counselor who might be able to help you deal with what happened to you."

The girl stiffened with a look of alarm.

"She's a woman, so she'd understand. She's helped a lot of other students."

"You mean other students have been raped?"

"No. But they've had other problems."

"Well, I don't want to talk with her."

"In case you change your mind," Maura said, "I can tell you where her office is."

"I don't want to know where her office is," the girl said, turning away and heading for the door. Without another word she bolted.

In her room that evening she talked with Solana about the girl's fear of her father believing that what those guys had done to her was somehow her fault.

"I can understand her fear," Solana said. "I wasn't in the same situation, but I had a reason to be afraid of what my parents would think of me."

Maura waited for her to explain.

"I never told this to anyone before, but I guess it's time I finally told someone. A few weeks after they killed Rafael, I discovered that I was pregnant."

"Oh, no," Maura moaned with sympathy.

"I was scared to death because sooner or later my parents would notice and then they'd know I made love with Rafael without being married to him. So I didn't tell them right away, I waited for the right opportunity. But then, before I could tell them, I lost the baby."

"Oh, no," Maura moaned.

"So I never told them. I didn't want to lay that burden on them for no reason."

"You bore it all by yourself."

"Yeah. I not only felt it was my fault they killed Rafael, I also felt it was my fault I lost the baby, even though I did everything in my power to keep it."

"Did that feeling drive you toward becoming a nun?"

"Well, I didn't want to have a baby with anyone else, so I didn't have a problem taking a vow of celibacy. And I wanted to make amends for the bad thing I did."

"From what you've told me," Maura said, "the only 'bad' thing you did was to make love with a man without being married to him. And almost everyone does that nowadays."

"If they hadn't killed him, I wouldn't have ever felt it was bad."

"So you worked back from the punishment to the sin."

"I guess I did," Solana said. "And I guess I did the same thing after I lost our baby."

"Have you gotten over the feeling that you were punished for making love with your fiancé?"

"Yeah. I've gotten over that feeling. But I haven't gotten over losing Rafael and then losing our baby."

"I understand. You know," she said after a pause, "Esperanza could be pregnant."

"Did she tell you she was afraid she was pregnant?"

"She didn't tell me, but when she talked about being afraid that her parents would find out what happened there was something in her voice that suggested it."

"If she *was* pregnant, what would you advise her to do?"

"Of course I'd advise her to have the baby."

"Do you think she'd consider having an abortion?"

"I don't think so. She's a good Catholic. But imagine what it would be like to have the baby of a guy who raped you."

"I can't imagine it," Solana said. "How could it feel like a blessing?"

"I don't know. But it happens every day—women are raped, and they get pregnant."

"But they don't always have the babies."

"From what I've read, they usually do. They don't have options."

"Well, let's hope that on top of everything else, the poor girl isn't pregnant."

"I'll pray that she isn't," Maura said. "I'll pray for mercy."

"I'll pray for that too," Solana said.

The next morning she was in her office when the receptionist called her and told her a student wanted to see her. Assuming it was Jeffrey wanting to know if she had given the locket to Esperanza, she told the receptionist to send the student in, but it was a girl she had never seen before, a tall lean girl with tied-back hair and intense blue eyes.

"I'm Wendy," the girl said. "Are you Sister Maura?"

"Yes," Maura said, not recognizing her as a student, but there had been so many over the years, and her memory wasn't as sharp as before.

"You never had me as a student, sister. I just transferred here this fall."

"Well, please sit down and tell me why you came to see me."

The girl sat down. Unlike most students she didn't slump, she had perfect posture even when sitting. "I understand that you're the head of the disciplinary committee."

"Yes, I am. Is there a matter you want to bring before the committee?"

Wendy nodded. "There is. It's a serious matter."

"Tell me about it," Maura said, wondering what it was.

"Instead of telling you, I'll show you," the girl said, taking out her smartphone. She moved a finger over the screen until she found what she was searching for. She held out the phone to Maura, saying: "This is a student."

There was a still picture on the screen, a picture of Esperanza whose eyes were closed as if she was asleep.

"Do you recognize her?"

"Yes. She's in my freshman seminar."

Wendy did something more on the phone, and she held it out again.

There was motion now, with the camera going down from Esperanza's face to her breasts, to her belly, and to her pubis, where it lingered for a while intrusively. And then it showed the girl splayed, gagged, and blindfolded.

"I have to warn you," Wendy said. "What you're going to see next is pretty gruesome."

Maura didn't want to see it, but she felt obligated to keep watching as a big guy covered the girl, and his bare buttocks started jerking up and down like a machine drilling for oil. He must have weighed about two hundred pounds, more than double what the girl weighed. And Maura could only imagine how much his brutal, relentless thrusting hurt her.

"I think that's enough for you to get the idea," Wendy said, pulling back the phone.

It was more than enough, and it left Maura in a daze of horror.

"That was a gang rape, and it happened on our campus."

"How do you know it happened here?"

"I'll show you," Wendy said. Again she moved her finger over the screen, and again she held out the phone to Maura. "You see that boulder?"

"Yes." It was a few yards behind Esperanza's head.

"Look at the graffiti on it."

There was a line drawing of a heart with two sets of initials inside it: "J.S. + R.M."

"I found that boulder. It's near the path that overlooks the river. It's in a wall of boulders that hides the spot from people walking by."

"You mean the spot where it happened."

"Yeah. I took a picture of it." Wendy did something more with the phone, and held it out to Maura. The screen was divided between the two pictures so that they could be compared, and it was definitely the same boulder.

"So you know it happened on our campus."

"I also know what they were doing before they attacked her."

"What were they doing?"

"They were drinking beer. They threw the empty cans into the woods, where I found them. You know how guys crumple empty beer cans? Well, they crumpled every one of those cans, I guess to prove how macho they were, so the cans have their fingerprints on them, not only from being held but also from being crumpled."

Maura understood. "Then you have evidence that could be used in court."

"I do, but I don't have any suspects, and I can't get the police to fingerprint every male student in the college."

"I gather you want to see those guys punished."

"Of course I want to see them punished," Wendy said with her eyes blazing. "They committed a major felony, and they should go to prison for it."

"Do you know the girl?"

"I know her now. I didn't know her before it happened. But after I saw that video I looked for her, and I found her."

"Do you know how she feels?"

"Yeah, I do. It happened to me."

"Did it happen at the college you transferred from?"

Wendy nodded. "That's why I transferred from that college and came here."

"Did the guys who raped you get punished?"

"No, they got off free. They were football players," Wendy added as if this explained why.

"Then you have a personal reason for wanting to see those guys punished. I mean, the guys who raped that girl."

"Whatever my reason," Wendy told her, "I want justice."

"Justice should be impersonal. When it's personal, it could be revenge."

"I don't want revenge, I only want justice. And I want those guys to go to prison so they can't rape any more girls."

"If that's what you want, then it's not a matter for the disciplinary committee. It's a matter for the criminal justice system."

"I have to start somewhere, and if the college expels those guys, then they won't have the opportunity to rape any more girls on our campus."

"But to take the matter to the disciplinary committee, you still need suspects."

"If you have a hearing on the matter, it might flush them out."

"Our hearings aren't public, so those guys wouldn't even know about it." Having said this, Maura admitted to herself that there could be a leak from the committee, and then those guys would know about it.

"Well, I think the administration of this college should know what happened. At least they could provide more security."

"You mean along that path."

"I mean generally. That's not the only spot on campus where a girl could be assaulted."

"I think you have a point, but we don't need a committee hearing to make a decision to provide more security. I can talk directly with the president about that."

"So will you talk with him about it?"

"I will," Maura said, knowing he would listen to her.

"You know," Wendy said after a silence, "I understand why Esperanza doesn't want to bring charges against those guys."

Maura waited, giving her a chance to continue.

"She doesn't want her parents to know what they did to her. But eventually they'll find out about it. Someone will tell them about this video."

"Someone will. And I've advised her to tell her parents before that happens."

"I'm glad you did. If she follows your advice, she won't have any reason not to bring charges against those guys."

"She won't have that reason," Maura said. "But she could have other reasons."

"She could, but they wouldn't be as strong."

"Did you tell your parents what happened to you?"

"I told them right away. I needed their support."

"Did they give you their support?"

"Yeah. They went to the police with me, and though we didn't get anywhere, they made me feel it wasn't my fault."

"Did you tell Esperanza how your parents supported you?"

"No. We didn't get that far."

"Well, you should tell her. It might encourage her to tell *her* parents what happened to her."

"Okay. I will," Wendy said as if she understood.

"And I'll talk with the president," Maura said, "about providing more security."

They shook hands, and for a long time after the girl left her Maura reflected, seeing how the various strands of the matter could be woven together to achieve the result that she hoped for. And it wasn't justice, it was mercy.

The president's office was in the mansion of the Morrissey family, who had donated their property to the sisters along with a substantial foundation for the purpose of establishing a college. On the outside the mansion still looked as it had in the middle of the nineteenth century, but inside it had been renovated to create offices for the top administrators. The president's office had been a den when the Morrisseys lived there, and it hadn't been changed much. It still had walls of built-in bookcases that included some tomes they had left behind.

The president was the first male in the college's history to hold that position and the third layperson. The first lay president was Frida, the stooge appointed by the chairman of the board of trustees who tried to sell the college's property for a real estate development. Frida was paid a high salary in return for carrying out the chairman's orders, and after the board finally replaced him and fired her she absconded with a large severance payment in return for keeping her mouth shut about his nefarious activities. The second lay president was Patricia, the financial wizard who after achieving five years of healthy surpluses and quadrupling the college's endowment left to assume the presidency of a large private university that needed her talents. The current president, Santiago, was not only the first male but also the first graduate of the college and the first Latino to hold the position. In fact, he had been a student in two of Maura's courses, so she knew him well, and as a member of the search committee she had strongly supported his candidacy.

Santiago was born in Cuba and came to Yonkers with his parents and an older sister when he was still a baby. His father had a business in Cuba that he lost when Fidel Castro took over, so he had to start over again. It took a while, but he built a successful business cleaning the offices of the corporate campuses and medical centers that proliferated in Westchester beginning in the Sixties. The family still lived in Yonkers, but they now had a house in the neighborhood near Sarah Lawrence College, which was virtually in Bronxville.

"Sister Maura," he said, coming out of his office to greet her. A perfect gentleman, he kissed her on each cheek in the Spanish fashion. "It's always a pleasure."

"For me too," she said, noting the first hints of gray in his hair. Whenever she saw former students years later she was reminded of how long she had been at the college.

"Please sit down," he said, gesturing to an area where there was a sofa and chairs. "Would you like some coffee?"

"No, thanks. If I have coffee late in the day, it keeps me up all night." She sat down on the sofa, while he settled into one of the chairs.

"So how are things going?" he asked, meaning things at the college. He valued her opinion on how well he was doing his job.

"I think they're going well. We increased retention by two percentage points over last year."

"I know. What do you think were the contributing factors?"

"Better academic advising, and better responses to our students' financial problems."

"Is there room for further improvement?"

"There's always room for further improvement."

"Well, you didn't come here to talk about retention," he said, shifting in the chair and opening the conversation to what was on her mind.

"No, I didn't. I came to talk about something that happened on our campus, which you should know about before it goes public."

"Okay," he said calmly. "What happened?"

"A girl in my freshman seminar was gang raped on our campus."

"Oh, my God." He bowed his head for a moment as if to pray for her, and then he asked: "How did you hear about it?"

"From the girl who was the victim, from one of the guys who assaulted her, and from another girl who wants to see the guys punished."

"So you have three witnesses?"

"The girl who wants to see them punished wasn't a witness, but she has a video of it."

"A video of it? Jesus Christ." Santiago brought his hand to his mouth and apologized, saying: "Excuse me, sister."

"That's how I felt when I heard about it."

"Where did that girl get the video?"

"The rapists made the video, using a smartphone."

"And they gave it to her?"

"No. They posted it on a website for gang rapes, where she spotted it."

Santiago shook his head sadly. "I guess I've lost touch with this generation. They gang rape girls, they make videos of it, and they post the videos on websites? How did we produce such bad kids?"

"The same way we always have—by showing them with our bad examples that it's all right to treat other people as objects. The only difference is that now they have a lot of technology to reinforce their behavior. But we're also producing good kids," Maura added. "So don't write off the whole generation."

"I won't. I just—" He stopped and didn't complete the thought. Instead, he resumed asking questions about her narrative. "How did you meet the girl who spotted the video?"

"She came to me. She has a mission to stop the violence against women on college campuses."

"It's a worthy mission. Did she tell you why she adopted it?"

"She was gang raped at a university where she was a student. She couldn't get any justice there, so she dropped out and came here, expecting better treatment of women."

"How does she know that this gang rape happened on our campus?"

"The video shows a boulder at the scene with graffiti on it that's identical to a boulder on our campus."

Santiago nodded grimly. "You said she wants to see the guys punished. I assume that means she wants them charged and tried in court."

"That's what she wants. But with all the evidence she has, she still doesn't have any suspects. The video doesn't show the faces of the guys."

"Did you watch the video?"

"I watched more than enough of it."

Santiago frowned. "Well, why hasn't the victim brought charges against those guys?"

"For one thing, they blindfolded her, so she didn't see their faces. And for another thing, she doesn't want her parents to know about it."

"She doesn't? Why not?"

"You have daughters."

"I have three of them, and they're gifts from God. Of course, they're not yet teenagers, so I could change my mind about that."

"Imagine how you'd feel if you found out that one of them had been gang raped."

"I'd be crushed," he said without hesitation. "And I'd be furious at the guys who did it. I'd want to see them put away for the rest of their lives."

"Would you blame your daughter in any way?"

"No. I wouldn't. If I knew she'd been gang raped, why would I blame her?"

"I don't know why, but are you sure you wouldn't blame her?"

Santiago considered. "I see where you're going. When a woman says she's been raped, people always wonder if somehow it was her fault."

"They do, including fathers."

"I understand. But if there's a video of this girl being raped, then sooner or later her parents will find out about it, won't they?"

"I think they will. So I've been trying to convince her to tell them what happened before someone else tells them."

Santiago leaned forward with his hands clasped. "Well, let's assume she does tell them. If I were her father, I'd want her to bring charges against the guys."

"Would you want her to appear in court?"

"I can see how that would be humiliating for her. But at least I'd want her to take the matter to the disciplinary committee."

"As president of the college, what do you want?"

"I want those guys expelled. We never should have admitted them."

"As far as I know," Maura said, "our admissions process doesn't have a filter for rapists."

"Then we should have some kind of test that detects guys who hate women."

"Maybe we should. But if we hadn't brought lacrosse to the college the guys who raped this girl wouldn't have come here."

Santiago frowned. "What do you mean?"

"I have reason to believe that the rapists are lacrosse players."

"But they could have been baseball players, or basketball players, or soccer players, or any guys who hang out together."

"I know. But in all the years I've been here, we haven't had a gang rape."

Santiago took a long deep breath and slowly exhaled as if they had talked enough about lacrosse players. "I want the matter to come before the disciplinary committee so that we can expel the assailants, whoever they are."

"The victim has to bring it to the committee."

"I know the process," Santiago reminded her, "and I hope she'll let you help her through it."

"I think she will eventually. And luckily I have someone who can identify her assailants."

"You do? Who?"

"One of the assailants. He's very sorry for what he did. In fact, he's feeling very deep remorse."

"Did this guy rape her?"

"No, he didn't. But he pinned her arms while the other guys raped her. And he wants to atone for what he did."

"How do you know?"

"He's willing to tell her parents what he did to her."

"You mean he's willing to tell her parents that he pinned their daughter's arms while three guys raped her?"

"He says he is. He went to the scene of the crime the next morning and found her locket there. He tried to return it to her, and when she wouldn't take it he asked me to return it to her. So I know he wants a reconciliation."

"Is that what you want?"

Maura nodded. "I don't want justice, though I can understand why the girl who showed me the video wants it. But I don't care about abstractions. I care about the two people who've been most affected by what happened. And I want to help them."

"You think it would help them if the matter went to the disciplinary committee?"

"I think it would. It would give the boy an opportunity to make a sacrifice for her, and it would give the girl an opportunity to forgive him."

"It's a complicated situation," Santiago said, "and I can see how it could go wrong. But I want what you want for those two kids, and I'll support you all the way."

"*Gracias*," she said.

He grinned. "Are you speaking Spanish now?"

"I've learned some words and phrases from Sister Solana."

"How's she doing?"

"She's doing fine. She's on the disciplinary committee, which could be helpful. The girl's Latina, so I think she'll feel more at ease with a Latina on the committee."

"I think she will. I know what it's like to go before a committee that has nothing but white people on it."

Before leaving his office she kept her promise to Wendy by asking the president to increase security on the campus, and having learned about the gang rape, he readily agreed to put more resources into security.

SEVEN

NOW THAT SHE had recovered the locket, Esperanza no longer had to lie about it to her mother, except to tell her she had found it under her bed. Having lost it, she cherished the locket more than ever, and though it hadn't protected her from those guys, she still believed in its power, and she hoped that something good would come from her recovering it.

Two days later something good did happen. When she took the pregnancy test again, it was negative, and that evening she started her period. She had never been so glad to have her period, and she said a prayer of thanks to Our Lady.

Since she believed that her not being pregnant greatly reduced the risk of her parents finding out what had happened to her, she was annoyed when the guy who had tried to return the locket to her approached her in the hall the next day and asked to talk with her. She was on her way to class, so it was easy to brush him off, but when she came out of the classroom an hour and twenty minutes later he was waiting for her outside the door.

"I need to talk with you," he said with a look of desperation in his eyes.

"We have nothing to talk about," she told him. "We don't even know each other."

"It'll only take about five minutes," he pleaded. "Do you have another class now?"

She didn't, and for some reason it was harder to lie to him than to her parents. "No, but I have to go and study."

"Just give me five minutes. Okay?"

She hesitated, not seeing how anything good could come from talking with one of her assailants, but almost against her will she said: "Okay."

"Let's go to the patio, where we talked before."

She went along with him, down to the cafeteria and out the door that led to the patio. They stopped at the edge, which overlooked the athletic fields—as before, the lacrosse team was practicing. She cringed at the sight of those guys in helmets and face masks running around with their sticks as if they were pursuing prey.

"I quit the team," he told her.

"You did?" She wasn't interested. She hadn't known that the sport of lacrosse existed until she went to college, and generally she didn't have much interest in sports, though she did join her father to watch the Mexican *fútbol* team playing in major tournaments like the Copa América.

"I'm glad to see you're wearing your locket," he said after a silence. "I gave it to Sister Maura so she could give it to you."

"I know. And thank you for returning it," she managed to say. She didn't look at him. She kept her eyes on the guys down on the field as if she was afraid they would storm up the hill and attack her.

"I want you to know how sorry I am for what I did to you. I'll never forgive myself."

She could tell without looking at him that he was crying, and her heart softened a little. But she said nothing to relieve him.

After a pause he asked: "Do your parents know about it?"

"No. They don't. And I don't want them to find out about it."

"But you must know about the video."

"Yeah. I know about it."

"I tried to stop them from posting it on that website, but they wouldn't listen to me."

She wondered if she was supposed to thank him for trying to stop them.

"So now everyone can see what happened to you, and sooner or later someone will tell your parents about it."

"I don't think so. The people in our community don't watch that kind of video."

"Maybe they don't, but the word will get around."

She turned to him in anger. "Why are you trying to upset me?"

"I'm not trying to upset you. I'm trying to help you."

"How could you possibly help me?"

"By supporting you when you tell your parents."

"I'm not going to tell them."

"But wouldn't it be better for you to tell your parents before someone else does?"

"No one's going to tell them about it."

"I hope no one does," he said as if he meant it, "but someone could, and then you'll wish you told them before."

"You don't know what I'll wish I did," she told him, trying to control her fear. "You don't know how I feel."

"I don't know, but I can imagine."

"You *can't* imagine. If you could, you wouldn't have pinned my arms while those guys—" She turned away from him, looking down on the field at the lacrosse players.

"I couldn't imagine then, but I can now."

"Why couldn't you imagine then?"

"I don't know. I knew what we were doing was wrong, but I just went along with them."

"If you knew what you were doing was wrong, you should have stopped them."

"I know I should have."

"You not only didn't stop them, you *helped* them rape me."

"I know I did. I'm really sorry."

"Well, let me ask you," she said, confronting him. "If I'd been a white girl, would they have treated me that way?"

"I think they would have. I think they would have found another reason to justify it."

"Then they hate girls, whatever their color?"

"I think they do. But I don't hate girls. I have two older sisters, who always loved me and cared for me. So I don't know why I went along with them."

"That's something you have to deal with. It's not my problem." She checked her watch and said: "You've had five minutes. And I appreciate your offer to help me, but I don't need your help. My parents won't find out about it."

"Are you sure?"

"I'm sure," she said, though she wasn't sure.

"Okay, but if your parents do find out about it, I can help you by supporting your story. And if you want to bring charges against those guys, I can identify them."

"I'll keep that in mind."

"Oh, by the way, my name is Jeffrey."

"I know your name. And I guess you know my name."

"I do," he said. "I should have known you'd know my name. We've both been talking with Sister Maura."

She headed back to the cafeteria, not waiting for him to accompany her. She wished he had let her alone. By reminding her of the video he shook the confidence she had gained from not being pregnant that her parents would never find out what had happened to her. And she began to worry again.

Instead of going home, she texted Griselda, and after verifying that her friend was in her room, she went to the dormitory, threading her way through a bunch of girls who were occupying the hall of the second floor. Griselda's door was open, so Esperanza knocked and went in.

"*Hola. Qué pasa?*" Griselda said, sitting at her desk.

"Well, there's good news and bad news."

"What's the good news?"

"I'm not pregnant."

"*Gracias a Dios!* That's very good news. You must be relieved."

"I am relieved. At least I don't have to tell my parents I'm pregnant."

"And what's the bad news?"

"The guy who tried to return my locket approached me again and asked to talk with me, and for some reason I let him."

Griselda waited for her to continue.

"He said he was sorry for what he did to me."

"You said he didn't rape you."

"He didn't rape me. But he pinned my arms while the other guys raped me. And while we talked he looked so miserable that I almost felt sorry for him."

"Almost?"

"Yeah, almost."

"So what does he want from you?"

"I think he wants me to forgive him. But I can't imagine forgiving him."

"Did he ask you to forgive him?"

"Not exactly. But he offered to help me. He reminded me of the video, and he said that sooner or later my parents will find out what happened. And he advised me to tell my parents before someone else does."

"I think that's good advice."

"It's the same advice that Sister Maura gave me. You know, he's been talking with her about it. He knew my name."

"Isn't that confidential information?"

"She's not a priest, and I don't mind her trying to help us. We both need help."

"So have you decided to take their advice?"

"I haven't decided anything yet. But I'm thinking about it. He offered to support my story."

Griselda's eyes were filled with awe. "You mean he offered to tell your parents he pinned your arms while three guys raped you?"

"He said he would."

"If a guy came to *my* parents and told them he pinned my arms while three guys raped me, my father would kill him."

"My father wouldn't kill him," Esperanza said. "He'd kill me."

"Oh, you don't mean that literally. Your father wouldn't kill you. He loves you."

"He loves me now, but he won't love me after he hears what those guys did to me."

"But you didn't let them."

"I know I didn't let them, but my father will think I did let them."

"Why would your father think you let them?"

"I don't know. I just think he would."

"But if he hears from that guy what they did to you, he'll believe you didn't let them."

"You mean he'll believe the guy, but he won't believe me?"

"The guy has no reason to lie about it, and he has nothing to gain by telling your father what he did."

"I guess that's true," Esperanza said, thinking about it. "While I have a reason to lie about it, and I have everything to lose by telling the truth."

Griselda shook her head adamantly. "You have everything to gain by telling the truth. If that guy supports your story and your father believes him, then you can stop worrying that your parents will find out about it."

"But what if my father doesn't believe him?"

"You mean your father will think you got this guy to lie about it because you had such a good time having sex with those guys?"

"I really don't know what he'll think. I only know what he'll feel. And I wish I could spare him from what he'll feel."

"What about your mother?" Griselda asked after a silence. "Won't she believe you?"

"Yeah, she'll believe me. She'll only say I should have known better than to walk on that path alone."

"But you were on a college campus, where you should have been safe."

"I know I was, and I felt safe."

"Well, I think you should tell your parents about it before someone else does. At least that way you'll have a chance to explain what happened before they make a judgment about it. And you'll have that guy to support your story."

"Okay. Well, thanks for listening."

"*De nada.* I'll pray to Our Lady of Altagracia that your father will believe you."

After talking with Griselda she felt a little better, and she resolved to tell her parents what had happened. She only had to contact Jeffrey so that he would be with her when she told her parents.

She figured it would be better to have him with her at that time instead of later when her father might already have made a judgment about it.

Jeffrey hadn't given her a way to contact him, but she assumed that Sister Maura would have his email address. Since it was after five now, she probably couldn't expect to find Sister Maura in her office, so she would have to go there in the morning and get the address. Or she could try emailing Sister Maura. The faculty all had email, and they encouraged students to use it. The problem was, most students didn't use email anymore, they used text messages, so that if Jeffrey didn't use email then Esperanza would need his phone number in order to contact him. But since most faculty didn't use text messages to communicate with their students, Sister Maura probably wouldn't have his phone number.

On the bus that took her downtown she emailed Sister Maura and asked for Jeffrey's email address and also his phone number, if possible. She didn't give a reason for her request since she assumed that Sister Maura would know why she wanted to contact him, and that she would be pleased that Esperanza was following her advice.

At home she found her mother in the kitchen, and she helped get dinner on the table for the three of them since her father was working at the restaurant that night. They had an uneventful dinner, and she was in her room studying when her father came home two hours earlier than usual. She heard him yelling at her mother, which he never did, and then she heard his steps coming toward her room.

He opened the door and slammed it behind him, saying: "*Señorita, tienes que darme una explicación.*"

"About what?" she asked, feeling her insides collapse with fear.

"About a video that shows you having sex with a lot of guys, one after the other."

"How did you see it?"

"That's not the point. The point is, I saw it."

"I need to know how you happened to see it," she insisted, terrified by the idea that her father watched videos of gang rapes.

"Don't talk to me that way," he said, slapping her face.

As far back as she could remember, he had never slapped her. He had never laid a violent hand on her. So it made her feel she was no longer his treasure, his gift from God.

She finally recovered from the blow and faced him, saying: "What you saw in that video was four guys raping me."

"Why didn't you stop them?"

"One of them grabbed me from behind and choked me until I was unconscious, and the next thing I knew they'd stripped me, gagged me, and blindfolded me. They held my legs, and they pinned my arms, so I couldn't stop them."

Her father looked as if he almost believed her.

"Where did it happen?"

"At the college."

"You mean they raped you in the middle of the campus?"

"It wasn't in the middle of the campus. It was near a path that overlooks the river."

"What were you doing there?"

"I was taking a walk, admiring the sunset."

"You were walking alone?"

"Yeah, I was on the campus. I felt safe there."

Her father shook his head as if he had a lot of questions about her story. "When did it happen?"

"About two weeks ago."

"Why didn't you tell us about it?"

"I was afraid you'd think I let them do it."

"Well, I don't know what to think," he muttered. "Your story is unbelievable."

"What's unbelievable about it?"

"That four guys attacked you in broad daylight on a college campus, and that no one was around to stop them."

"No one could see what they were doing. They were hidden from the path by some huge boulders."

"You say you didn't let them have sex with you," her father said as if he was trying to connect her story with what he had seen on the video. "You say they raped you."

"They did, and if you don't believe me, I have a witness who will support my story."

"You mean someone who watched it happen?"

"No, someone who participated."

"One of the guys who you say raped you?"

"He didn't rape me," she said almost as if she was defending him. "He pinned my arms while the other guys raped me."

Her father grimaced. "You expect me to believe a guy who you say pinned your arms while the other guys raped you?"

"Why would he lie to you?"

"I don't know." Her father looked at her suspiciously. "Maybe you asked him to lie."

"If you listen to him, you'll know he's not lying."

"Why would he come and tell me about it?"

"Because he's sorry for what he did."

"Okay," her father said after a silence. "Have him come here and tell me about it. I'm off work on Monday and Tuesday."

"I'll contact him."

"*Bien.*" Her father started to turn away from her.

"Before you go," she said, "will you tell me how you happened to see the video?"

"Why does it matter?"

"It matters because I don't want to think you watch videos of gang rapes."

Her father raised his arm as if he was going to slap her again, but he held it back, saying: "Fair enough. And I don't want you to think I watch videos of gang rapes."

She waited for him to tell her.

"Last week I had to fire a kitchen worker. He took too many breaks, and he just wasn't doing his job. So tonight he came to the back door and asked for me. I thought he was looking for his final paycheck, so I went outside to see him. And he had one of those smartphones, which he shoved into my face, saying my daughter was a *puta.*"

"Did you watch the whole thing?"

"No. After seeing enough, or more than enough, I knocked the phone out of his hand, and I stomped on it. I went to get a knife, and I was going to cut his throat, but they stopped me. They told me to go home."

"Do they know what he showed you?"

"No, they don't. They only know we had an argument about something."

She had an idea. "I don't want you to see any more of it, but if you'd watched the whole thing you would have seen what the leader did to me after they were finished."

"What did he do to you?"

"*Él hizo pis en mí.*"

"*Hijo de puta! Le cortaré el pene!*"

Encouraged by his reaction, she said: "If you know anything, you know I didn't let him do that. So how could you believe I let them rape me?"

Her father recovered his composure and said: "I'll let you know what I believe after I've heard what this guy has to say."

She was hoping that her father would reach out and caress her head as he often did, but he left the room without touching her. It made her feel he didn't want to soil his fingers on her, and it broke her heart.

A while later her mother came into her room and said: "He told me everything, and I believe you. But you have to understand how he feels."

"Does anyone understand how *I* feel?"

"I understand how you feel," her mother said. "It never happened to me, but it happened to one of my friends, so I have some experience with it."

"Then maybe you can explain to me why I feel that somehow it was my fault."

"The world makes us feel that way. When things happen,

someone has to take responsibility, and men never do, so women take responsibility."

"But I'm not going to take responsibility for what those guys did to me."

"I'm not saying you should. I'm only saying that the world makes you feel like you should."

"Then we need to change the world."

"We do. But in the meantime we need to stop letting the world make us feel like we should take responsibility for the things that men do."

Esperanza thought about it. "So I should stop letting *papá* make me feel it was my fault?"

"Yes, you should."

"But why does he blame me for what happened?"

"What he saw in that video hurt him deeply. You're the reason why he's in pain."

"But it wasn't my fault."

"I know it wasn't," her mother said. "And I think he *knows* it wasn't your fault. But he still *feels* that somehow it was."

"Well, the guy who pinned my arms while the other guys raped me is willing to come here and support my story."

"You father told me."

"Do you think it would change how *papá* feels?"

"I think it would help. At least it would give him someone else to direct his anger at."

"Well, I don't want him to kill the guy."

"Your father won't kill him. But be prepared for an explosion."

When her mother had left her she checked her email and found a message from Sister Maura. It gave her Jeffrey's email address, and she immediately sent him a message, saying: "My parents found out about it. Someone showed the video to my father. He doesn't believe my story, so I need your support. My father's off work on Monday and Tuesday. Would either of those evenings work for you?" After sending the message she was struck by the incongruity of asking for support from a guy who had pinned her arms while three guys raped her, but she felt as if he was her only hope.

That night she lay awake thinking about her father. In some ways his reaction wasn't as bad as she had feared, but in other ways it was even worse, especially when he slapped her. The blow had taken her down from the level where she had always imagined herself in his eyes to the level of an unruly child who needed to be smacked in order to correct her behavior. Recalling how she had talked to her father, she felt he was justified in slapping her, which reinforced her feeling that what those guys had done to her was somehow her fault.

But then she remembered why she insisted on knowing how he happened to see the video. If he watched videos on a website for gang rapes, he couldn't be the father she had always known. She realized now what a crazy idea it was, but at the time it had terrified her. If her father was on the side of those guys, she couldn't look to him for support, and she couldn't be sure that in the long run her mother would stand up to him.

As she lay there she kept returning to the fact that although she had made some progress with him, especially when she told him what the leader did to her when they were finished, he still didn't quite believe her story. Was it because, as her mother had said, they lived in a world that made women take responsibility for things that men did? If that was truc, did it extend to all the terrible things that men did to women?

Refusing to accept such a world, she decided to stand firm in the position that it wasn't her fault, and maybe then, with Jeffrey's support, her father would believe her.

When she woke up the next morning she checked her messages, and she found an email from Jeffrey that said either day would work for him, so she told him Monday, wanting to get it over with as soon as possible.

Later that morning she had a class with Sister Maura, who treated her like the other students but approached her at the end of class and asked: "Do you have a minute?"

"Yeah. Sure." She waited for the classroom to empty.

"Did you reach Jeffrey?"

"I emailed him, and he replied. I told him to come to our apartment on Monday. The problem is, my father found out about it yesterday."

"You mean before you could tell him about it?"

"Someone showed him the video."

"Oh, Lord." Sister Maura raised her eyes to heaven.

"He acted like he believed I let those guys have sex with me, and I kept trying to make him understand that I couldn't stop them."

"He couldn't see from the video that you were overpowered?"

"I guess he couldn't. He could only see that I let those guys have sex with me."

"Please stop saying that. Those guys didn't have sex with you. They committed an act of violence against you. They held you down and they raped you."

"I know they did."

"I think your father's stuck in his first impression of what happened. If he really thinks about what he saw, he'll realize that you weren't having sex, you were being raped."

"Well, maybe Jeffrey can help him to realize that."

"Let's hope he can. At least he'll give your father someone else to direct his anger at."

"That's what my mother said. But I can't understand why he's angry at me. What did I do to him?"

"You destroyed his image of you as a pure young woman."

"But I didn't destroy his image of me. Those guys did."

"As long as he believes to any extent that it was your fault, he'll be angry with you. So you need to work on what he believes."

"I understand. As I told you, Jeffrey's coming to our apartment on Monday, and I hope he can make my father believe it wasn't my fault."

Sister Maura paused as if to consider the situation. "Well, I think it's a good sign that your father's willing to listen to him."

"Yeah. I just don't know how my father will react when Jeffrey tells him what he did. I'm afraid that my father will hit him."

"Does your father hit people when he's angry?"

"He hit me. I mean, he slapped my face."

Sister Maura frowned as if this wasn't a good sign. "What made him do that?"

"I insisted on knowing how he happened to see the video."

"Why did that matter to you?"

"It mattered because I had a crazy idea that my father watches videos of gang rapes, and it terrified me."

Sister Maura looked puzzled. "Do you have any reason to believe that your father watches videos of gang rapes?"

"No. But does he have any reason to believe that I'd let those guys have sex with me?"

"You're right. We don't need reasons for believing things. But please stop saying they had sex with you."

"My father didn't see the violence," Esperanza said, "he only saw the sex. So I think it's appropriate in that context."

"Maybe it is, but for the love of God, please don't say it to describe what they did to you."

"Okay. I won't." She checked her watch. "I have to go. And thanks for caring about me."

"I'm not the only one who cares about you," Sister Maura said with a hopeful look in her eyes. "Your father and your mother care about you."

"I know they do," she said as an act of faith.

She left the classroom feeling better. But she still worried about how her father would react to Jeffrey, and whether having Jeffrey support her story of what had happened would convince her father that it wasn't her fault. Beyond that meeting, she couldn't see what else she could do to convince her father.

EIGHT

HE EXPECTED THAT Sister Maura would ask to talk with him after class on Friday, but when it was over she caught his eye with an unspoken question, and knowing what it was, he nodded, meaning yes, he was going to meet with Esperanza's father. And Sister Maura let him go, evidently believing she didn't have to advise him on how to handle the meeting.

That afternoon he learned that his new room would be available the next morning, so he started getting his things together in anticipation of the move. The college supplied the basic furniture so most of the things he had to move were clothes and books. Since his roommate had gone home to Long Island for the weekend, Jeffrey had the room to himself, and before he went to work at the restaurant he piled his things on Kenny's bed.

The next morning he moved into his new room. It took him several trips, but within a few hours he was settled there, and knowing he wouldn't be able to concentrate, instead of studying he walked to St. Brigid in the hope of talking with Father Paul.

The priest wasn't in front of the church with a cigarette, so Jeffrey went in and stopped and listened for voices from the confessional, but there was only silence—he couldn't even hear the usual recorded chants in the background. He was wondering if Father Paul had gone to St. John's Hospital to visit parishioners who were patients there when he heard the sound of a door opening, and the priest appeared.

"I knew you were here," Father Paul said, approaching him purposefully.

"How did you know? Do you have surveillance cameras?"

Father Paul laughed. "No, I just have feelings. And I had a feeling you were here."

"But isn't there a difference between knowing and having a feeling?"

"There is, but we can bridge the gap."

"You mean with faith?"

"Yes. Faith is the realization of what is hoped for, the evidence of things not seen."

"That's a quotation from someone, isn't it?"

"It's from my namesake, in his letter to the Hebrews."

"I thought it sounded familiar."

"Well, you didn't come here to talk about scripture," Father Paul said, moving toward their usual pew. "Would you like to sit down and bring me up to date?"

They sat down in their usual places.

"I gave the locket to Sister Maura," Jeffrey began, "and she gave it to Esperanza. I saw her on campus a few days ago, and I got her to talk with me."

"Was she wearing the locket?"

"Yeah, she was. She thanked me for returning it."

"That's a good sign."

"I offered to support her story if she told her parents what happened to her, but she still believed they wouldn't ever find out about it, so she declined my offer."

Father Paul waited as if he knew what was coming next.

"That night she emailed me saying that her parents had found out about it, and that her father didn't believe her story, so she needed my support."

"How did she get your email address?"

"She must have gotten it from Sister Maura."

"Did she tell you how her parents found out about it?"

"Someone showed the video to her father."

"Oh, Lord. We really didn't need that to happen."

"She told me her father's off work on Monday and Tuesday," Jeffrey continued, "and I told her either of those evenings would work for me, so we agreed on Monday."

"To get it over with sooner?"

"Yeah. It'll be the hardest thing I've ever had to do."

"It will be. So have you thought about what you're going to tell her father?"

"No, I haven't. I'm only going to tell him the truth."

"Of course you're going to tell him the truth, but you should focus on how you guys overpowered Esperanza and prevented her from resisting or crying for help."

"So I should describe how we gagged her, blindfolded her, and held her down?"

"Yes, you should. It must have been in the video, but he missed it because he only saw his daughter having sex with those guys. So you need to give him the details and make him believe it wasn't her fault."

"But I wonder," Jeffrey said, "if he didn't believe what he saw in the video, why would he believe me?"

"He didn't see the details, he only saw his daughter having sex."

"I hope he understands that I have no reason to lie about what happened to her. I mean, I'm sticking my neck out by admitting what I did."

"You are. You could go to prison for what you did."

"Do you think I *should* go to prison?"

"If you truly repent," Father Paul told him, "and if you do everything you can to help Esperanza deal with what happened to her, then I don't think you should go to prison. You can pay for what you did in other ways."

"Well, one way is to tell her father what happened to her and convince him that it wasn't her fault."

"I hope you're successful. I'll pray for you."

Father Paul accompanied him out of the church and stopped in front and took out a cigarette, which he carefully lit.

After lingering for a moment Jeffrey thanked him and left him, heading back to the college. As usual, it had helped to talk with the priest. He knew what he had to tell Esperanza's father, and as he walked north on Broadway he began to prepare what he would say.

He spent the rest of the day studying and catching up on his assignments. When he had done enough, he thought about going home. He hadn't seen his parents since they had left him at the college before the beginning of the semester, and he would have liked to see them. But he had to work that evening and also on Sunday, so it just wasn't possible for him to take the train to Poughkeepsie and back within his work schedule. In any case he wasn't ready to tell his parents what he had done since he didn't yet know its consequences.

That night, his first at the college without a roommate, he realized that he would pay for what he did by being alone, cut off from people who hadn't done evil things of the same order of magnitude as what he had done. He was isolated from people who hadn't committed mortal sins or major felonies. At the same time, he was isolated from people who *had* committed mortal sins or major felonies but felt no remorse. That left a small number of people in the world with whom he might find company. Ironically, the only person with whom he had a relationship now was the victim of his sin, his crime. And if he failed to convince her father, he wouldn't have even that relationship.

Of course he would still have his parents and his sisters. But he was afraid that when they found out what he had done, they wouldn't want to have anything to do with him, especially his sisters, who would regard him as a monster.

For most of the night he lay awake castigating himself for going along with those guys. If he had fought them, it might have given the girl a chance to get away. Or if he had threatened to call the police, it might have made them realize that they could get into serious trouble for what they were about to do. At the very least, he should have refused to pin the girl's arms, which would have left her free to hit them or kick them since there would have been only two guys to hold her legs and arms while the other guy raped her. But by going along with them he had enabled them to rape her, just as whoever had pinned the arms of Jesus had enabled them to drive the nails into his hands.

On Monday morning he forced himself to get out of bed and go to class. He had gotten very little sleep, and he was exhausted from his ordeal. He wished he had told Esperanza that he would meet with her father on Tuesday, but it was too late. He already had an email from her asking him to meet her in the cafeteria at five so that they could take the bus together.

He arrived at the cafeteria about ten minutes early, and he didn't see Esperanza there. He did see Brandon, Scott, and Kenny at a table with some girls who looked impressed with them. Of course the guys had their sticks, which rose above the table like swords at a council of war. Before Jeffrey could turn away from them, they spotted him, and derisively Brandon made his stick go up and down.

They kept an eye on him, and when Esperanza arrived they all made their sticks go up and down, whooping with delight.

"Do you know those guys?" she asked him, giving them only a sideways glance.

"I played lacrosse with them," he told her, "before I quit."

"They're very rude."

"Yeah, they are."

They left the cafeteria without another word and headed for the bus stop. When they got there she said: "I live in South Yonkers. It's about fifteen minutes by bus."

"That's fine." He didn't know what else to say.

"As I told you," she said after a silence, "someone showed the video to my father, and he exploded."

"I don't blame him."

"Well, I blame him for believing it was my fault."

"I'll tell him what happened."

"But when he watched the video, he should have seen that I was overpowered."

"You didn't watch the video, did you?"

"No, but it must have shown that I was gagged, blindfolded, and held down by three guys."

"It must have," he said, painfully conscious of having been one of those guys.

The bus arrived within a few minutes, and they rode in silence downtown and into an area where he had never been before.

When they got off the bus he felt as if he was in a foreign country, though the signs on stores were mostly in English.

"This is my neighborhood," she told him almost with pride.

Not knowing what else to say, he asked: "Have you lived here your whole life?"

"Yeah. We lived in a building farther south until about two years ago when we moved into an apartment with three bedrooms."

"You have a brother or a sister?"

"I have a brother. He's still in high school."

"I have two sisters. They're both older."

"If you have two sisters—" she began, but she stopped without finishing the thought.

He guessed it would have been: "How could you have done what you did?"

They stopped at a building and she took a key out of her pocketbook and unlocked the door. He followed her up three flights of stairs with his eyes fixed on the heels of her feet. He smelled tomatoes and onions cooking.

He followed her into an apartment, right into the living room where a man was sitting on a sofa, watching soccer on television. The commentary was in Spanish.

"Hi, Dad," she said with a catch in her voice. "This is Jeffrey."

Her father uncoiled like a spring and rose from the sofa with his fists clenched. He was only about five feet six, but he was solid, and he looked as if he could hold his own in a street fight. He reminded Jeffrey of the Mexicans who worked in the kitchen of his father's restaurant, except that he was older and better dressed.

"I'm glad to meet you," Jeffrey said without thinking about it.

Surprisingly, her father extended his arm and shook his hand as if they were just two people meeting.

"Should I get Mom?" Esperanza asked, fingering her locket nervously.

"Yes, she should hear this," her father said, and then to Jeffrey: "Please sit down."

Jeffrey sat down in a chair that was facing perpendicular to the sofa, in a position either to watch television or to talk with a person on the sofa.

A woman who was shorter than Esperanza came into the room, wiping her hands on an apron. Her eyes were very anxious.

"Mom, this is Jeffrey."

"I'm glad to meet you," Jeffrey said again.

After shaking hands the woman sat down in the chair opposite the one in which Jeffrey had taken, while Esperanza sat down on the sofa, leaving the middle cushion empty between her and her father.

They all kept their eyes on Jeffrey as he began: "What I'm going to tell you is really awful, and if you get angry, I won't blame you."

Her father nodded and motioned for him to go ahead.

"About two and a half weeks ago I went with three of my teammates from lacrosse—"

"Lacrosse?" her father said. "What's that?"

"It's a sport that was originally played by Native Americans."

"I never heard of it. They play it at the college?"

"Yeah. They haven't played it long there. I think only for a few years."

"So you went with your teammates—"

"We went on the path that overlooks the river to a place where we could drink beer."

"Drink beer?" Her father looked puzzled. "I thought you were on a sports team."

"I am. I mean I was. We only practice in the fall. We play our games in the spring."

"Okay. You went to a place where you could drink beer."

He took a deep breath, and he braced himself for what was coming. "After a few rounds one of the guys spotted your daughter on the path alone, and he told our leader."

"Did you see her on the path?"

"No. I didn't see her. We were hidden from the path by some huge boulders."

"Then how did this guy spot my daughter?"

"He went into the woods to pee, and when he came out he spotted her."

"What happened then?"

"Our leader went up to the path, and the next thing I knew, he was carrying your daughter on his shoulder. She was unconscious, so he must have gotten her in a chokehold."

"Are you sure she was unconscious?"

"Oh, yeah. She didn't know what was happening to her." He took another deep breath. "They laid her down, and they took off her clothes."

"Did you help them?"

"No. I only watched them while they gagged her with her panties and blindfolded her with her shirt. But when they asked me to pin her arms I went along with them. I don't know why." By now he could no longer stop himself from crying.

After a moment her father said gruffly: "While you were pinning her arms, what were the other guys doing?"

"They were holding her legs, one on the right and the other on the left."

"So she couldn't hit them or kick them."

"No. She couldn't do anything to stop them."

Her father looked at Esperanza with a glimmer of sympathy.

"I could have stopped them," Jeffrey said, "but I didn't even try. I let them rape her, one after the other. I enabled them to rape her."

"Did *you* rape her?"

"No, I didn't. I swear I didn't."

"He didn't," Esperanza confirmed.

"How do you know?" her father said. "According to your story you were blindfolded, so you couldn't see them."

"I recognize his voice. When one of the other guys told him it was his turn, he said he didn't want to, and he didn't."

"But he pinned your arms so the other guys could rape you."

"Yeah, he did."

"*Maldito cabrón!*" her father snarled, leaping from the sofa and pouncing on him.

The chair fell over backwards, and his head hit the floor. It didn't knock him out, but it made him see stars. Her father was immediately on top of him, squeezing his neck with his hands and saying: "I'll show you a chokehold."

Her father was strangling him.

"*Para, papá!*" Esperanza screamed.

"Why should I stop? He deserves to die for what he did."

"But it won't help to kill him. It'll only make things worse."

Her father finally loosened the hold, and Jeffrey was able to breathe again. He sat up on the floor and said: "Your father's right. I deserve to die for what I did."

"I should have killed you, and I would have killed you if Esperanza hadn't stopped me. So why did you stop me?" her father demanded, turning on his daughter.

"I didn't want you to commit a mortal sin."

"Are you sure you were only concerned for me?"

"I was also concerned for him."

"You were?" Her father looked at her suspiciously. "You know, when you asked me to stop, you sounded like you care about him. Is there something going on between you and him?"

"There's nothing going on between us."

"Then why did he come here to support your story?"

"Because he's sorry for what he did."

"Oh?" her father said, raising his eyebrows. "You know how he feels?"

"I don't know how he feels, but I can imagine how he feels."

"He pinned your arms while three guys raped you, and you can imagine how he feels?"

"Yeah, I can imagine how sorry he is," Esperanza said, standing up to her father.

"You can? So you expect me to forgive him?"

"No. I only expect you to believe him."

"Why should I believe him?"

"Because he's telling the truth."

"Hmm," her father muttered, shaking his head. "Well, I don't know if I believe him. I need to think about it. So please get this *bola de mierda* out of my sight."

Jeffrey rose to his feet, and without saying another word he followed Esperanza out the door and down the stairs.

They stood for a moment in front of the building, and then she said: "Thanks for trying."

"Do you think he'll believe us?"

"I think he might. But I have a feeling that he'll want something more from us."

"What more could he want?"

"I don't know, but I can imagine."

In his mind he followed her to the logical next step of the process, but he didn't say it. He only told her again: "I'm sorry. I'm so sorry."

She looked as if she knew how he felt.

That evening he was in his room studying when there was a heavy knock on his door. He knew who it was, so he said: "Come in."

Brandon led the way, followed by Scott and Kenny.

"Hey, this is a nice room you have," Brandon said, looking around.

"A private room," Scott said. "What luxury."

Jeffrey was still sitting at his desk, and they were circling around him menacingly.

"We saw you today with that little spic," Brandon said, tapping him on the shoulder. "What were you doing with her?"

"I was just talking with her," Jeffrey told him.

"Are you sorry you didn't take your turn with her?"

"We don't have that kind of relationship."

"Oh? What kind of relationship do you have?"

"We're classmates, that's all."

Brandon scowled. "That's *all* after what you did to her?"

"She doesn't know what I did to her."

"Then why's she hanging out with you?"

"I don't know. I guess she likes me."

"How did you meet her?"

"We have a class together."

"Well, if you knew her, why didn't you say something when you saw me carrying her from the path?"

"I didn't know her then."

"Oh. But you know her now?"

"I've gotten to know her since then."

"Why have you gotten to know her? You like spics?"

"You have a problem with them?"

"Yeah, I do. They're taking over our country. They come here illegally, and they live on welfare while we support them with our taxes."

"Are you a taxpayer?"

"My father's a taxpayer. He pays a lot of taxes, which mainly go to those people."

"You don't know what you're talking about. You should get some real information before you repeat what other people say."

"You know what I think?" Scott said. "I think that girl wants something from you."

"What could she possibly want from me?"

"She could want you to identify us."

"For what purpose?"

"Don't act dumb," Brandon said. "So she can bring charges against us."

"Well, if that's what she wants, I can't stop her."

"You could stop her by not identifying us."

"If she asks me to identify the guys who did it, I'm not going to pretend I don't know."

"But you just told us she doesn't know what you did to her," Scott said. "So why would she ask you to identify us?"

"Maybe you were lying about that," Kenny said.

"So tell us the truth," Brandon said. "Does she know what you did to her?"

Realizing that if he told them the truth they might do something to prevent Esperanza from bringing charges against them, he said: "No. She doesn't know."

"Well, she better not find out."

"What would you do if she did find out?"

"We'd kill her," Brandon said as if her life didn't matter.

The threat made him feel he had done the right thing by protecting her. But it also made him realize that the only way to protect her in the long run was to get the truth on record before they could stop him.

The next day he waited for Esperanza outside the classroom where she had the freshman seminar with Sister Maura. When she saw him there she didn't look surprised.

"We need to talk," he told her.

"I know. I was going to look for you."

"Did something happen at home?"

"Yeah. My father made a decision. I can't talk about it here."

They went to the usual place on the patio outside the cafeteria. The athletic field below was empty now except for a maintenance man who was touching up a line.

He waited for her to speak first.

Staring bleakly across the river, Esperanza said: "My father decided that he'll believe our story only if I bring charges against you guys."

"Does he want you to go to the police?"

"He wants me to go to the disciplinary committee, and if they rule in my favor he'll be satisfied. If they don't, then he wants me to go to the police."

"Does he realize how hard that'll be for you?"

"He has no idea. But I'll do anything to make him believe it wasn't my fault."

He understood, and he responded to her need, saying: "I'll help you. I'll identify the other guys, and I'll support your story all the way."

"Thanks," she said in a low voice.

"We have to start the process."

"You mean before those guys rape another girl?"

"I mean before they do anything to stop us from testifying against them."

She looked concerned. "Did they threaten to do something?"

"Yeah, they did. So we have to get the truth on record."

"Okay. But if the committee rules in my favor, you'll be punished along with those other guys."

"I know I will. I deserve to be punished."

"Well, I hope they're not too hard on you. Without your help I couldn't have dealt with this."

"Without my help," he said with remorse, "they couldn't have raped you."

Now that they were definitely going to have a hearing at the disciplinary committee, Jeffrey could no longer put off telling his parents what he had done. The last thing he wanted was for them to find out in a letter from the college informing them that he had been expelled for a disciplinary matter. So after checking the train schedule he phoned his mother and told her he was taking the Amtrak from Yonkers that arrived in Poughkeepsie at three forty-five. He explained that he wanted to bring them up to date on things at the college.

His mother was at the station with her car. He planned to wait for an opportune time to talk with both his parents together, so as they drove from the station up to their house he only made small talk, which began with a question on how the restaurant was doing.

"Your father's there now," his mother said, "but he's going to take the night off so we can be together with you."

"That's good," he said, inferring that his mother knew he had something important to tell them, though she couldn't have imagined what it was.

"We'll have dinner at home. I bought scallops from the fish market."

He was touched by her treating him to his favorite seafood, and that made him feel even worse about what he was going to tell them. He decided to wait until after they had eaten so at least it wouldn't spoil their dinner.

The small talk extended through the dinner with his responses to questions about how things were going at the college. From the way they acted, he realized that his parents knew that something was wrong, and that they were waiting for him to tell them about it.

After dinner they retired to the living room, where his father settled in an easy chair with a glass of brandy and his mother sat down in the other chair, with Jeffrey on the sofa. Reminded of the scene at Esperanza's apartment, he drew from the script he had followed there, beginning with the four teammates going to drink beer at a spot off the path that overlooked the river.

"Oh, my God," his mother said when he got to the part where one of the guys brought the unconscious girl to the spot. "Please tell us you didn't hurt her."

When he told them how he had pinned the girl's arms, his father said: "It can't be true. You couldn't have done such a thing."

"Well, I did," he said. "I pinned her arms while the other guys raped her."

His father made a choking sound as if he was going to throw up.

"Did *you* rape her?" his mother asked.

"No, I didn't. But I enabled the other guys to rape her."

"*What the hell was the matter with you?*" his father raged. "Were you on drugs?"

"No, I wasn't on drugs. I was only a little tipsy from drinking beer. But that's no excuse."

"What *is* the excuse?"

"There's no excuse."

"I just can't understand why you did it," his mother said with tears in her eyes. "We certainly didn't raise you to hate women."

"I don't hate women."

"Then why did you do it?"

"I don't know," he wailed in despair.

"We failed you," his mother sobbed. "I don't know how, but somehow we failed you."

"You didn't fail me. I failed myself."

There was a long silence, except for the sound of his mother sobbing.

"For no reason," his father finally said, "you completely lost your moral sense."

"You know, what you did is a mortal sin," his mother said.

"It's also a major felony," his father said.

"I know. I'm sorry. I'm so sorry." Before, he was sorry for the pain he caused the girl, but now he was also sorry for the pain he caused his parents. And he realized that in a way he had hurt his parents as much as he had hurt the girl.

"Did you make a confession?" his mother asked.

"I talked with a priest about it, but I didn't make a formal confession."

"What kind of priest," his father asked, "would let you off from a formal confession?"

"I also talked with a nun about it. She's trying to bring about a reconciliation."

"Between you and God?" his mother asked.

"No, between me and the girl."

His father choked on the brandy he had taken a drink of. "That nun actually believes she can bring about a reconciliation between you and the girl?"

"Yeah. The thing is, the girl needs me to make her father stop believing it was her fault."

His father frowned. "If she was overpowered by four big guys, how could her father believe it was her fault?"

"If that happened to one of your daughters," his mother said, "would you believe it was her fault?"

"Of course I wouldn't."

"You're forgetting how you reacted when Elizabeth got into trouble. You believed it was her fault."

He had no idea what they were talking about. Whatever had happened to his sister, it was a closely guarded family secret.

"Okay. But I had to make sure it wasn't her fault."

Trying to make a connection, Jeffrey said: "I think that's what her father wants—to make sure it wasn't her fault."

"So how's her father going to do that?"

"By having her bring charges against us."

"He wants her to go to the police?"

"No, he wants her to go to the college's disciplinary committee, and if they rule in her favor, he'll be satisfied."

His father paused for a moment to think. "What role do you have in that process?"

"I'm the only person who can identify the other guys. They blindfolded her so she never saw their faces."

"How did she identify you?"

"I identified myself to her. I went back to the scene of our crime, where I found a silver locket that one of the guys ripped from her neck, and I returned it to her."

"Why did you return it to her?" his mother asked hopefully.

"I realized that it was something of value to her. Inside the locket was a picture of Our Lady of Guadalupe."

"So she's Catholic."

"Yeah. Her family's from Mexico."

"If she has an older brother like the guys in my kitchen," his father said, "he'll kill you for sure. They're very protective of their sisters."

"She only has a younger brother, who probably won't ever know about it."

"If she goes to the police, then it'll become public knowledge."

"Yeah, I know. That's why we hope it ends with the disciplinary committee."

"If they rule in her favor," his mother asked his father, "how do you think the college will punish him?"

"They'll expel him," his father said.

"If he cooperates, won't they be lenient on him?"

"That's not why I'm supporting her story," he said. "I'm supporting her story so her father will believe it wasn't her fault."

"I understand that," his father said. "But think about yourself. If the college expels you for what you did, then no other college will ever accept you."

"I wouldn't go that far," his mother said.

"If you were the president of a college, would you want a guy on your campus who pinned the arms of a girl so that three other guys could rape her?"

"If he took his courses online as Elizabeth did, he wouldn't be on a campus."

"Okay. He can get a degree online. Or he can go to work and forget about college."

There was another long silence.

Finally his mother said: "What you did was a mortal sin, and you have no excuse for it. But you're still our son, and since you're truly sorry for it, you have our support."

"You have our support all the way," his father said. "If you need a lawyer, we'll get one for you."

"Thanks," he told them, wiping his eyes. "But I don't want a lawyer. I mean, I don't want to get off lightly. I want to pay for what I did."

"That's well and good, but if this matter goes to court you could get five years."

"Well, maybe it won't go beyond the disciplinary committee."

"I hope it doesn't. But keep us posted."

"I will," he said, feeling that the conversation was over.

Before he went to bed his mother gave him the usual hug, saying: "I'll pray for you. I'll pray for that girl. And I'll pray for a reconciliation."

NINE

MAURA WAS IN her office, sitting at her desk and grading papers. She had noticed that Jeffrey was waiting in the hall for Esperanza after class, and she was encouraged by the fact that they were talking with each other. She wondered if Jeffrey had already gone to the girl's home to support her story with her father, and if that effort had been successful. If it had been, then Esperanza wouldn't have the same motive for bringing the matter to the disciplinary committee, but at the same time she wouldn't be deterred as she was before by the fear that her parents would find out about it. Maura had two purposes: to bring about a reconciliation between Jeffrey and Esperanza, and to rid the college of the guys who had raped Esperanza. She put a higher priority on the reconciliation, but even if bringing the matter to the disciplinary committee was no longer necessary for that purpose, it was still the only way of expelling the rapists.

"Do you have a minute?" a voice asked her from the doorway.

She turned and saw it was Esperanza, who must have slipped by the receptionist, or else the latter had taken a break. "Yeah, sure. Come in."

The girl came in and sat down in the usual place, setting her backpack on the floor.

"Did Jeffrey talk with your father?"

"Yeah. And it helped, but my father still feels it was somehow my fault. I mean, he still has doubts. So he wants me to go to the disciplinary committee."

"Will that satisfy your father?"

"He says it will if they rule in my favor."

"What if they don't?"

Esperanza sighed. "If they don't, then he wants me to go to the police."

"How do you feel about going to the committee?"

"I know it's going to be hard for me, but I'll do anything to make my father believe it wasn't my fault."

"Then the first step is for you to file a formal complaint."

"You mean in writing?"

"Yes. You don't have to go into all the particulars, you just have to state what they did to you, and that you didn't consent to it."

"How many pages does it have to be?" Esperanza asked as if it was a term paper.

"It shouldn't take more than two pages. Double spaced," Maura added. She stopped short of specifying Times Roman twelve font.

"Will you review it and correct my English?"

"Yes, I will. But the statement has to be in your own words. I can't write it for you."

"I understand. When do you need it?"

"The sooner, the better. If I get it tomorrow, I can return it to you on Thursday."

"Okay. But there's a problem," Esperanza said after a pause. "Except for Jeffrey, I don't know who the guys were."

"You don't have to name them in your complaint. In fact, since you didn't see their faces you can't name them. You can only say what they did to you. But at the hearing, Jeffrey will name them. He witnessed what they did to you."

"If the committee rules in my favor, will he be punished too?"

"Of course. He participated in what they did to you."

"But he didn't rape me," the girl reminded her. "He only pinned my arms."

To test the sympathy for Jeffrey that she detected, Maura said: "If he hadn't pinned your arms, they couldn't have raped you. So he's as guilty as they are."

"I know he is. But for some reason I don't feel he is. Does that make any sense?"

"I think it does. What makes him different from the other guys is that he's sorry for what he did. He's truly sorry."

"I can tell he's sorry. And he's been trying to make amends. I mean, by returning my locket and by talking with my father."

"So how did your father react when Jeffrey told him what they did to you?"

"My father attacked him and began to strangle him, and he would have killed Jeffrey if I hadn't screamed at him to stop. But that's what made him have doubts again. It made him think there was something between us."

"You mean between you and Jeffrey?"

"Yeah. And of course there isn't. I only screamed because I didn't want my father to kill him. If he had, he would have gone to prison and we would have been deported."

"You're a U.S. citizen. You can't be deported."

"Well, you never know. There are people who will do anything to get rid of us."

Deciding not to pursue that issue, Maura said: "Now, I need to understand your father's thought process. He thinks that if there's something between you and Jeffrey, then maybe you consented to what those guys did to you?"

"I don't know. I guess that's how he thinks. I don't understand how men think."

"I don't either. Most of the time they don't think, and that's the problem. If those guys had stopped to think even for a moment, they wouldn't have done what they did to you."

"You know what's not fair," Esperanza said after a silence. "When you do the right thing and people take it the wrong way."

"Can you give me an example?"

"Yeah, I can. Screaming to stop my father from killing Jeffrey was the right thing to do, but he took it the wrong way."

"You mean instead of understanding that you wanted to stop him from committing a mortal sin, he got the idea that there was something between you and Jeffrey."

"That's exactly what I mean."

"Well, it happens," Maura said, "and it's not fair. But that shouldn't ever stop you from doing the right thing."

The girl lingered, and then she asked: "When I write my statement, should I email it to you?"

"No, you should give it to me directly. You don't want to leave a trail for anyone."

"Okay. I'll bring it to you tomorrow."

As she watched Esperanza go out the door her heart was rent by the feeling that this innocent kid had to deal not only with male brutality toward females but also with male distrust of females. Though there had been a few improvements, the world was still patriarchal, as evidenced by the fact that females were being kidnapped and sold into slavery, and raped, and tortured, and killed wherever males rampaged, which was nearly everywhere, even on the campus of a Catholic college. It roused the dormant feelings that had almost made Maura leave the order in protest against the conservative reaction to the reforms of Vatican II and the adamant refusal of the hierarchy to allow women to play a greater role in the church. But now as head of the disciplinary committee she would have a chance to redress at least one injustice.

Before she left her office Maura emailed Jeffrey asking him to meet with her the next day. She didn't hear back from him until the next morning. He said he was on the train coming back to Yonkers from Poughkeepsie, and he asked if he could meet with her around eleven. She replied saying that eleven would be fine. By now she knew he was from Poughkeepsie, and she assumed he had gone there to tell his parents what he had done. She could only imagine how his parents reacted to learning that their son had pinned the arms of a girl while three other guys raped her. It made her glad she wasn't a parent.

Jeffrey arrived on time and sat down where Esperanza had sat the day before. He looked as if he hadn't slept last night.

"Did you go home?" Maura asked him.

"I went there yesterday to tell my parents."

"How did it go?"

He took a long deep breath and exhaled, saying: "It made me feel that in a way I hurt them as much as I hurt Esperanza."

"In a way you probably did. But I've never been a parent, so I really don't know."

"Well, I have their support. They didn't disown me."

"That's good. Do they know you're going before the disciplinary committee?"

"Yeah, they know. My father said that I'll be expelled, and that no other college will ever accept me."

"If you *are* expelled, then you won't have many choices. But according to Esperanza, you're committed to the process."

"Yeah. So tell me what I have to do."

"I need a written statement from you describing what you did to Esperanza and identifying the guys who raped her."

"Do you need a lot of details?"

"No. I need what happened and who did it."

"I could give you a statement right now."

"I need it in writing. You could use my laptop if you want to."

"Okay. I want to get it on record now."

She detected an urgency in his tone. "Are you worried that those guys will try to stop you?"

"They've already tried. But I'm not worried for myself, I'm worried for Esperanza."

"Did they threaten to do something to her?"

"They threatened to kill her."

"So you think that if you get it on record they won't have any reason to kill her?"

"If it's on record and they kill her, the police will know who did it, so killing her would only get them into worse trouble."

Maura was impressed. "Have you thought of majoring in criminal justice?"

"No, I want to work in the restaurant business like my father."

"Here," she said, pushing her laptop across the desk. "I'll leave you for a while. I'll be back in a half hour, okay?"

"Okay," he said, turning his chair and moving it closer to her desk.

"If you sit at my desk, I think you'll be more comfortable."

She left the office and wandered around, looking for colleagues to gossip with. She stepped into the office of the new assistant professor whom they had hired to teach theology, and she killed about twenty minutes discussing the Pope's encyclical *Laudato Si'* which had shown her how the Catholic Church might play a role in saving the planet. And then she returned to her office, where she found Jeffrey sitting in her chair and gazing sorrowfully at the screen of her laptop.

"Are you done?" she asked him.

"Yeah, I'm done. I just need to print it."

"Do a print command. It'll go to a printer."

He pressed some keys, and then he vacated her chair and sat down in the other chair.

The printer, which she shared with other faculty, was outside her office in the hall, so she went and retrieved what he had printed. She had read most of it by the time she returned to her chair behind the desk. She had already heard what they did to Esperanza, and she had even seen parts of the video that showed what they did to her. What was new was the identification of the other guys, two of whom were students in her business ethics class—the guys who came late, carrying their lacrosse sticks. And she wasn't surprised.

"I know Brandon and Scott," she said. "I don't know Kenny."

"Those are the guys. Esperanza didn't see their faces, but she should recognize their voices. She recognized mine."

"If this is your statement, then you have to sign it."

"No problem," he said, taking the pen she offered him.

She watched him sign the statement feeling as she had many years ago at a railroad station as she watched the wheels of a steam locomotive starting to turn.

Handing back her pen, he asked: "Can you tell me when they'll begin the process?"

"I haven't worked out a schedule yet, but I expect to begin next week. The only problem is finding a time when everyone can meet together."

After Jeffrey left her office she heard him talking in the hall with Esperanza, who a few minutes later arrived with her statement, saying: "I hope this is all right."

"If you can wait, I'll review it now."

"Yeah, I can wait."

She read the statement. The content was fine, though there were a few grammatical errors. Instead of correcting them Maura decided to leave them since they would undermine any claim that the statement had been written for Esperanza by someone else.

"Is it all right?"

"Yes, it's fine. You just need to sign it." She offered the same pen to Esperanza, who signed the statement carefully.

"He told me you'll begin the process next week."

"That's what I'm hoping," Maura said, taking it as a good sign that they had exchanged this piece of information.

"Well, I just want to get it over with."

"We all do. I'll let you know when I have a schedule."

An hour later she was sitting on the sofa in the president's office waiting for him to get off the phone. From his respectful tone of voice, it sounded like he was talking with the chairman of the board of trustees. She pretended not to overhear the conversation, though from the words that filtered through she gathered they were talking about the dormitory project.

"Sorry," he said after hanging up the phone. "That was Chase."

She knew he didn't mean the bank, he meant the chairman of the board, who was one of those people with a last name for a first name. The only thing Maura knew about him was that he had made a lot of money on Wall Street and had gained his position at the college by donating a lot of money, including a major amount to refurbish the athletic fields. That project was being held up by a debate whether to have natural or artificial turf.

"He wanted to know if the dormitory project is on schedule," Santiago said, settling into a chair that faced the sofa.

"Is it?" Maura asked, having wondered why it was taking so long to lay the foundation.

"Oh, yeah. In fact, it's ahead of schedule."

"That's good to know." She paused and then said: "Remember the gang rape?"

"How could I forget about it?"

"Well, the girl is bringing charges against the guys."

"I thought she didn't know who they were."

"She still doesn't know, but the guy who pinned her arms identified them. He gave me a statement an hour ago."

Santiago frowned. "I thought she didn't want her parents to know about it."

"She didn't, but they found out about it. Someone showed the video to her father."

"Jesus," Santiago gasped, rolling his eyes. "Excuse me, sister."

"As I explained before, she didn't want her parents to know about it because she was afraid that her father would believe it was somehow her fault, and unfortunately she was right. He did believe it was somehow her fault. And even after the guy who pinned her arms went to her father and confirmed her story, her father still felt it was somehow her fault. So that's why she's bringing charges against them."

"To prove to her father it wasn't her fault?"

"That's right. She's going to the disciplinary committee, and if they rule in her favor, then her father will be satisfied."

"What if they don't rule in her favor?"

"She'll have to go to the police."

With his elbows resting on his knees, Santiago clasped his hands and leaned his forehead against them, thinking or praying or maybe doing both. For a long time he said nothing, and then he asked: "How do you think it's going to come out?"

"I think the committee will rule in her favor."

"Why do you think that?"

"I have a statement from the victim describing what happened. I have a statement from one of the participants that identifies the other three guys. And I have the video."

"You have the video?"

"Well, I don't actually have it, but I can get it," Maura said, knowing that Wendy had it.

"Do you think I should watch it?"

"You mean as the president of this college or as the father of three daughters?"

Santiago grimaced. "I was thinking of that first role, but you're right to point out that other role. So what do you think?"

"I think you should watch it in both roles. You should know what goes on at the college, and you should know what kind of world your daughters will have to deal with."

"I hope you're not suggesting we have gang rapes at the college every day."

"No, but we have other forms of harassment every day. And they're caused by the same attitude toward women."

"You suspected it was lacrosse players. Were you right?"

"Yes. The four guys are lacrosse players."

"Well, I still think it's absurd to believe that lacrosse players are more capable of committing acts of violence than soccer players or baseball players."

"I don't believe they are."

"So you don't have a bias against lacrosse players?"

"No, I don't. I just don't think the sport belongs at our college. It's for rich, white people in the suburbs, and those aren't the people we serve."

Santiago nodded as if he agreed. "Do you think you can give those guys a fair trial?"

"Of course I can. I'll be as fair to them as I would be to any guys who gang raped a girl."

"You sound like you've already reached a verdict."

"I have," Maura said. "And when you see that video you'll reach a verdict. There's simply no question about it."

"Then why have a hearing?"

"Because the college has a process for disciplinary matters."

"Should we involve the college attorney?" He was referring to a young man who after graduating from law school couldn't find a job so had joined the college in some kind of legal capacity. He was somehow related to a board member.

"We don't need him. The process is given in the committee's by-laws, so we just have to follow that."

"Okay, sister. It's in your hands."

Back in her office she emailed Wendy asking for a copy of the video. Wendy replied saying she would bring the video later today and asking if she also wanted the beer cans. Maura said yes, she could use the beer cans and also the photos of the boulder with the graffiti.

Wendy arrived with a plastic shopping bag, which she set on the desk, saying: "Here are the beer cans. I was careful not to get my fingerprints on them. And the photos of the boulder with the graffiti are in the bag."

"Thanks," Maura said. "Please sit down."

"Is she going to the police?" Wendy asked after sitting down.

"No, she's going to the disciplinary committee."

"Well, I hope she doesn't stop there."

"She might, depending on what the committee decides."

"If she does stop there, then the worst thing that can happen to those guys is to be expelled."

"But would sending them to prison do any good?"

"Yeah, it would do a lot of good. It would punish them for what they did, and it would make an example of them."

"It would punish them," Maura agreed. "But it might not rehabilitate them."

"I don't want to rehabilitate them. I want to see them put away so they can't rape any more girls."

"But they wouldn't go to prison for life."

"They deserve life. They even deserve the death penalty. You know, we used to give the death penalty for rape."

"I know. And that would certainly stop them from raping any more girls. But would it stop other guys from raping girls?"

"Yeah, I think it would stop them."

"I don't think it would. I think it would take something else to stop them."

"What would it take?"

"It would take learning not to treat other people as objects."

Wendy shook her head, saying: "I don't think guys are capable of learning that."

"I think they are," Maura said, undeterred by the intransigence of Wendy's position. "At least some guys are capable of learning from their mistakes."

"Can you give me an example?"

"Yeah. The guy who pinned Esperanza's arms while the other guys raped her."

"I don't know him, but if he pinned her arms while they raped her he's as guilty as they are."

"He *is* as guilty as they are, but we weren't talking about guilt. We were talking about him being capable of learning."

"So what makes him different from the other guys?"

"He's deeply sorry for what he did, and he's trying to make amends for it."

"But how could he *ever* make amends for what he did?"

"That's a good question. And I have to be honest, I don't know. But he's trying to make amends, so I have to give him credit."

"You sound like you're grading him," Wendy scoffed.

"I'm not grading him. I'm trying to help him learn."

"Okay. So the guy learned from his mistake. But did Esperanza learn from what those guys did to her?"

"That's another good question."

"She didn't make a mistake, did she?"

"I can't think of any mistake, except believing she was safe on a college campus."

"Aren't girls supposed to be safe on a college campus?"

"They are, and we should make them safe."

"You could make them safe by not admitting guys."

"We used to be a college for women. But there were always guys around, so not admitting them wouldn't be a solution."

"I wasn't serious. I was just telling you how I feel about them."

After a silence Maura said: "You asked if Esperanza learned from what those guys did to her, and I didn't have an answer. I still don't. But I think she's learning from what happened since then, as people learn from what happens after a disaster."

"I hope you're not saying it was good for her."

"Oh, not at all. It would have been better for her if it had never happened. But it did happen, and she's learning from the process of dealing with it. I think she's already learned a lot, and she's only at the beginning of the process."

"What has she already learned?"

"She's learned that no matter what happens, there's always a possibility of reconciliation."

"I don't believe that," Wendy said. "There's no way I could ever have a reconciliation with those guys who raped me."

"It doesn't have to be with them. It could be with other guys."

"You mean I should consider the possibility that all guys aren't like those guys?"

Maura nodded. "That would be a start."

There was a long silence, and then Wendy said: "Oh, I haven't given you the video. I brought two copies in case you need more than one."

"I do need more than one," she said, intending to give a copy to the president.

Wendy handed her two flash drives, which she had taken out of her pocketbook. "Do you know where to plug them into a computer?"

"Of course I know where to plug them. You'd be surprised by what nuns know about computers."

Wendy smiled. "Well, let me know if I can help you in any way. And thanks for what you said about reconciliation. It's something I should think about."

When the girl had gone Maura found the number of the police station on Shonnard Place, where the captain was a graduate of St. Catherine. He had been her student years ago, and he was a useful contact in situations that potentially involved the police. He was the kind of police officer who believed that his job was keeping people out of trouble rather than locking them up after they got into trouble.

When he got on the phone, which took a while, she told him she had evidence that might have to be used in a trial. She explained what it was, and she asked him if they could take fingerprints off it for possible matching with the fingerprints of guys who had committed a crime. As an alumnus of the college, he understood that she was hoping to resolve the matter without a trial, and he agreed to send a man over and pick up the beer cans.

With that done, she got the file on the disciplinary committee, which hadn't met in over a year. The last matter was a case of cheating, and it had been easy to resolve. They put the student on probation and warned him that if he cheated again he would be expelled.

The committee had seven members. Its by-laws stipulated three faculty members, two administrators, and two students. The faculty were elected at large, the administrators were the director of student services and the director of student activities, and the students were the president of the student government and the student representative on the academic affairs committee. After reviewing the list of current members Maura was satisfied with the diversity of the committee in terms of gender, race, generation, ethnicity, and religion. There were four females and three males. There were four whites and three nonwhites. There was one baby boomer, four gen-Xers, and two millennials. There were two Italian-Americans, two Latinos, one Irish-American, one African-American, and one whose ancestors probably came from Germany, based on his name. There were five Catholics, one Protestant, and one Jew.

The challenge was finding a time when they could all meet. There was a software program that you could use to find out when people were available, but no matter what people said, committees often ended up meeting on Fridays since that was the day when faculty and students were most likely to be free. So instead of going through that process, Maura decided to schedule the meeting for noon the following Friday. She verified that the boardroom in Morrissey Hall was available at that time, and she composed an email to notify members of a special meeting of the disciplinary committee to deal with a very urgent matter. She offered lunch as an inducement for them to attend. After reading over her email, she hit the button to send it.

Then she left her office and headed back to the convent, feeling a sudden need for a nap. It was only during the past few years that she had begun to feel such a need around the middle of the afternoon. Before, she had gone from five in the morning to eleven at night without any rest, but since she had turned eighty she had slowed down a little, though she still worked about twice as many hours per day as her students did. Evidently, they were still experiencing developmental processes that required eleven hours of sleep, whereas even now—except for the occasional need for a nap—Maura did fine with only six hours of sleep.

She made it to her room without being cornered by anyone, and after setting her alarm clock, which wasn't necessary in the morning, she lay down for a half hour and actually slept for fifteen minutes. After getting up she went to the chapel and prayed for the usual list of people, which now included Esperanza and Jeffrey and, as a last-minute addition, Wendy. She also prayed for the wisdom it would take to guide the committee.

At dinner she arranged with Solana to meet later that evening. Solana was one of the three faculty on the committee, and she needed to be brought up to date.

They met in Maura's room, with Solana in the only chair and Maura on the edge of the bed. Maura was sipping Dewar's on the rocks when Solana arrived, and she offered some to Solana, who shook her head, saying: "I don't drink Scotch. I only drink Dominican rum."

"What brand? I'll have it for you next time."

"Brugal. That's what my father drinks."

"How *is* your father?"

"He's fine. But he doesn't have enough to do. He's driving my mother crazy. He should have kept working."

"That's why I keep working," Maura said. "I don't want to drive people crazy."

"You already drive some people crazy."

"You mean the guys who think there's no place for women in the church."

"I'm waiting for the pope to say more about that."

"Yeah, I am too." She sipped her drink. "I assume you got my email about the meeting."

"I did," Solana said, "and I have a question. Since I was the victim of a gang attack, I'm wondering if I should be recused."

"Because you couldn't be impartial?"

"Yeah. I'll be on that girl's side."

"But wouldn't you be on her side anyway?"

"As a woman, or as a Latina?"

"As a human being."

Solana considered. "I guess I would be. But couldn't you find someone to replace me who has less reason to be on her side?"

"It would have to be someone who hates women."

"Well, that wouldn't be hard to find."

"Yeah, I'd only have to look among the church hierarchy."

They both laughed.

"If this was a jury," Solana said seriously, "they'd recuse me right away."

"It's not a jury. It's a committee."

"Yeah, I know. But it's going to make decisions that will affect people's lives."

"We make those decisions every day. When we fail a student, it affects her life."

"It's supposed to, but sometimes I wonder."

"I know what you mean. Anyway," Maura said after taking another sip of her drink, "there's no provision in the by-laws of this committee for replacing a member who might have a conflict of interest."

"There isn't? Well, there should be."

"Then after this case we'll revise the by-laws."

Solana was silent for a while, and then she said: "I understand that the purpose of this committee is to decide if students have broken a rule of the college. But this case goes way beyond that kind of thing. It's not about plagiarism or cheating."

"You're right. It's not."

"Have we ever had a case like this before?"

"We really haven't. The worst case I remember was about stealing from the bookstore."

"There's a commandment against stealing," Solana said. "But what about rape?"

"You know," Maura said after thinking about it, "there isn't a commandment against rape. There's one against adultery, and one against coveting your neighbor's wife. But there's nothing specific about committing rape."

"So I guess we've made progress since those commandments were written."

"I don't know. We still have a lot of men raping women."

"But at least now there's a law against it."

"There is, but I read somewhere that only five percent of all rapes are ever reported, and only a small percent of those result in convictions. So the law against rape isn't any more effective than the law against sending text messages while you're driving."

Solana shook her head in condemnation of this reality. "What made the girl finally decide to bring charges against those guys?"

"Her father found out what happened to her, and he believes it was somehow her fault."

"I understand, though I didn't have that problem with my father. But if he'd known the full extent of my relationship with Rafael, I might have had that problem."

"What happened to you was different from what happened to Esperanza. Your fiancé was killed, whereas she was raped. And you were attacked by a gang on the street, whereas she was attacked by lacrosse players on a college campus. So even if this case went before a jury, you might not be recused."

"The particulars were different. But what happened to me and that girl was essentially the same thing. It was male violence against a female."

"I understand. But if every victim of male violence was recused from the juries that make decisions on these cases, there wouldn't be many females on the juries, and I wonder if justice would be done."

Solana nodded. "Then I shouldn't be recused. The committee needs me."

On Friday, an hour before the first meeting of the committee, Maura got a call from the police captain at the Shonnard station, who gave her some information that would be very useful if the matter went to court. She thanked the captain and filed the information in her brain, where she could retrieve it if for any reason she needed it.

Then she went to the boardroom, and with the help of a student worker she set up her laptop at the foot of the table so that she could project onto a screen behind the head of the table. And she tested the projection, showing part of a video that she used in her business ethics course.

The first arrivals were the two students: Juan, the president of the student government, and Diane, the student representative on the academic affairs committee. They were both seniors, and both had taken Maura's junior seminar. She remembered that Juan was majoring in health science and that Diane was majoring in accounting. She told them to help themselves to the food, which the guy from the cafeteria had brought shortly after she got there. She had insisted on normal sandwiches of tuna salad, chicken salad, roast beef, and ham and cheese instead of the wraps they were always pushing. The students piled their plates with sandwiches and potato salad, as usual amazing her with the quantities of food that they could eat.

Solana arrived next and took one half of a sandwich and sat down to the right of the head of the table, where Maura wanted her. She was followed by John, the director of student activities, and Francesca, the director of student services. The last to arrive, almost ten minutes late was Myron, the other faculty member, who taught in the psychology program. He was a popular teacher, and he acted as if he had enough student votes to do whatever he pleased at the college. Of course it wasn't unusual for faculty to be late for meetings, as Maura had learned from having served as dean for the school of liberal arts. Faculty, who were the least busy of any of the college's constituents, tended to have the most difficulty in finding a time in their schedules to attend a meeting.

Maura took a roast beef sandwich for herself and sat down at the head of the table. They all made small talk until they had finished eating, and then Maura got their attention, saying: "Thanks for coming. I know you'd rather not have meetings on Fridays, but this was the only time when we could all get together. Looking ahead, I expect to need at least five meetings for this case, so if you can also meet on Wednesdays, that would speed things up. Who's not available at noon next Wednesday?"

Juan raised his hand. "I have a dentist appointment then."

"Please change your appointment to another day. Does anyone else have a conflict?"

"I have another meeting at that time," Myron said, "but if this meeting is more important—"

"It's more important. Please reschedule your other meeting."

There were no other conflicts, so Maura continued. "So we'll meet next Wednesday at noon, next Friday at noon, and for two weeks on Wednesday and Friday at noon. Okay?"

"Okay." They proceeded to input that information into their smartphones.

"We haven't met for a while," she told them, "so I want to remind you that everything you hear or see at our meetings is absolutely confidential. That means you can't tell *anyone* about the case. You can't tell your wife, or your husband, or your boyfriend, or your girlfriend. You can't tell anyone. Is that clear?"

They nodded in silence.

"Is someone going to take minutes?" John asked her.

"Yes. Are there any volunteers?" She knew from experience how reluctant people were to take minutes at meetings, so she waited only a decent interval before saying: "John, will you take the minutes?"

John, the only Protestant, was more in awe of nuns than the Catholics were, and he was always respectful to her. "Yes, sister."

"Thank you," Maura said. "Now, I want to warn you. What you're going to see is extremely unpleasant. It's an act of utter brutality, committed against one of our students. And I'm sad to say, it happened on our campus."

They waited tensely for her to continue.

"I'm going to show you a video of what happened."

"Someone took a video of it?" Francesca said in disbelief.

"Yes, someone did. Not only that, he posted it on a website for gang rapes."

"There's a website for gang rapes?" Diane said with wide eyes.

"There's probably more than one such website," Myron said as if he knew what people did on the internet.

Maura got up and moved to the foot of the table and sat down at her computer. "Solana, could you turn off the lights?"

Solana got up and flicked a switch.

Maura activated the video, which began with a girl lying unconscious on the ground. Maura had only seen the parts that Wendy had showed her, so now she was going to see the whole thing, and she braced herself for it.

Two guys, whose faces you couldn't see, took the girl's clothes off. One of them stuffed her panties into her mouth and then tied her shirt around her head, gagging her and blindfolding her. Then two guys each grabbed a leg while another guy pinned her arms with his knees.

"I don't want to watch this," Francesca said.

"You have to watch it," Maura said. "You have to see what happened to her."

They followed the action through three successive rapes, and then the final indignity. At that point John jumped up from the table holding his hand against his mouth. With bulging eyes he bolted from the room, presumably heading for the bathroom.

When the video ended there was a silence, a very long silence.

Finally Myron asked: "How do you know that happened on our campus?"

Maura got out the two photos of the boulder that Wendy had given her. She showed them to Myron, saying: "This photo is from the video, and this one was taken later at the scene of the crime. It's the same boulder."

Gazing at the photos, Myron asked: "Where is this?"

"It's off the path that overlooks the river."

"Have you been there in person?"

"No, I haven't. I got these photos from a student."

"Well, I think we should all go to the spot and see that boulder."

"Okay," Maura said, thinking it was a good idea. "We could all use some fresh air."

They were filing out of the boardroom when John returned with moist eyes.

"Are you all right?" she asked him.

He nodded. "Yeah. I'm sorry I ran out, but it made me sick."

"I know," she said, patting him on the shoulder.

"How could they have done that to her?"

"That's a good question, and I don't know the answer. I don't think I'll ever know the answer. Come on, we're going to the scene of the crime."

She walked with him, following the others. They headed across the athletic field, led by the students, who evidently knew about the path. They walked along the path and then down into the hollow. They looked at the boulder with graffiti on it.

"It's the same boulder," Myron said, holding the photo from the video.

"So it happened here," Francesca said. "It happened on our campus."

Maura looked around the hollow, thinking of the women who had gone to the cave where Jesus was buried. There they had seen evidence of his resurrection and run joyfully to tell their colleagues about it. But here Maura saw no evidence of a joyful event. She only saw evidence of a crime in which an innocent kid had been brutally assaulted, degraded, and humiliated. And she fervently prayed: "Lord, have mercy!"

TEN

ESPERANZA WAS SITTING at the kitchen table, trying to eat breakfast. Her gut was in knots, and nothing would go down, so she kept sipping water, hoping it would soothe the eruptions from her stomach. But every time she thought about having to go before the disciplinary committee she felt a stab of fear, and she curled up in pain.

Returning to the kitchen in her scrubs, ready for work, her mother advised her yet again: "*Simplemente diles la verdad.*"

"I will. But what if they don't believe me?"

"Don't worry. They'll believe you." Her mother put her arms around her and held her close. "Our Lady of Guadalupe will protect you."

"She didn't protect me a month ago," Esperanza said with her face pressed against her mother.

"She did. She stopped them from killing you."

"Sometimes I wish they *had* killed me."

"Don't talk like that. Your life is a gift from God, and you should be thankful for it. Your father and I are thankful for it."

"I bet he wishes I'd never been born."

"He doesn't wish that. He only wishes that this terrible thing had never happened to you. But it did, and we all have to deal with it."

"Do you think that if they rule in my favor he'll finally believe it wasn't my fault?"

"I know he will," her mother said, rubbing her back in a circular motion. "So just tell the truth, and everything will be fine."

She stayed at the table for a while after her mother left for work. She still couldn't eat anything, but she knew she couldn't concentrate if she tried to study, so she just sat there, staring into space and trying to remember what life had been like before those guys attacked her. She had trouble relating to the girl she had been before it happened.

At ten thirty she got on a bus that would take her to the college. As it approached her stop she felt like staying on and going wherever the bus went, anywhere but the college.

But she got off where she was supposed to, and she walked slowly into the campus. Checking her watch, she saw that she had an hour to kill before the meeting, so she went to a secluded area where the nuns could enjoy a view of the river in privacy. Students weren't supposed to go there, but since she felt that her need outweighed the rule, and since no one else was there, she sat on a bench and gazed at the Palisades, praying: *"Dios te salve, María, llena eres de gracia."*

She arrived at Morrissey Hall about fifteen minutes before she was due there, and she sat in the reception area, waiting to be called into the meeting. Her gut was still in knots, but she was determined to hold herself together, and silently she repeated her mother's advice like a mantra: "Just tell the truth, just tell the truth."

"Esperanza," the receptionist told her. "You can go in now."

At that moment the door was opened by Sister Maura, who let her pass, saying to her in a low whisper: "Don't worry. You'll be all right."

There was a long wooden table around which the members of the committee were sitting. She didn't recognize any of them.

Sister Maura introduced her to them and asked her to sit at the foot of the table. The student members were sitting at that end of the table, a compact Latino guy and a big white girl. She was embarrassed by their knowing what had happened to her.

"Esperanza," Sister Maura said, "we want you to tell us what happened to you on the afternoon of Wednesday, October 7. If you like, you can start by reading your statement. Did you bring a copy?"

"No, I'm sorry. I didn't think of it."

"It's all right. I have a copy." Sister Maura handed a folded paper to the Latina woman sitting at her right, who sent it down the line to her.

She unfolded the paper.

"We'll let you read the whole statement before anyone asks a question. Okay?"

"Okay." She began reading, and she was glad that Sister Maura had let her start by reading her statement since it gave her something to lean on, which she needed badly. She was so nervous that her right leg was shaking.

She got through the statement without looking up from the paper, so she had no idea how the members of the committee had received what she told them.

"Thank you, Esperanza," Sister Maura said. "Are there any questions?"

"I have a question," the Latino guy said. "When you went for a walk along that path, what time was it?"

"It was around five."

"Did you feel safe alone on that path in the evening?"

"Yeah, I felt safe. I was on a college campus. I wasn't in my neighborhood."

"If students don't feel safe on our campus," the black man said, "then we have no right to bring them here."

The Latino guy nodded as if he was satisfied.

The big white girl raised her hand, and Sister Maura called on her.

"Why didn't you fight them off?" the girl asked, implying that if she had been in Esperanza's position she would have fought them off.

"There were four of them," she said, "and they were big guys."

"Could you tell us how much you weigh?" the black man asked her gently.

"I weigh ninety pounds."

He looked at the committee members. "Do you know how much lacrosse players weigh?"

"I don't know," the white man with freckles said. "But I'd guess they weigh about a hundred and seventy-five pounds."

"The average weight of those four guys is a hundred and eighty-five pounds. I got that information from the roster," the black man added.

The man with freckles did a quick calculation. "So those guys had seven hundred and forty pounds against her ninety pounds."

"That's my point. And I think it answers Diane's question."

Diane didn't argue with him but she looked as if she still had doubts.

"I have a question," the Latina woman said. "Why did it take you so long to report what those guys did to you?"

"I didn't want my parents to know about it."

"But you must have needed their support."

"I did need their support. But I was afraid that my father would believe it was my fault."

The man with freckles nodded as if he understood. "There are a lot of studies on that problem. When females are victims of male violence they often feel it was their fault."

"That's not exactly what she said," the white woman with glasses said. "She said she was afraid that her *father* would believe it was her fault."

"She was afraid that her father would believe it was her fault because she felt it was her fault, and she projected her feeling onto her father."

"In my experience," the Latina woman said, "you don't have to project doubts onto a man in that situation. Men always have doubts about women."

"I agree with you," the white woman with glasses said.

"Whatever the underlying reason," Sister Maura said, wanting to get them back on track, "Esperanza was afraid that her father would believe it was her fault."

"And he still feels it was my fault. That's why I'm here—to convince my father that it wasn't my fault."

"I don't want to belabor the point," the black man said, "but there were four guys, weighing a total of seven hundred and forty pounds against this girl's ninety pounds. So there was no way she could have fought them off."

The man with freckles said: "We understand why you couldn't fight them off, and why it took you so long to report what they did to you. And we understand why you finally brought the matter before this committee. But do you have any other reason for bringing it before us?"

"What do you mean?"

"Do you want those four guys to be punished for what they did to you?"

"No, I don't," she said honestly. "I only want to get back into the good graces of my father."

"I understand," the Latina woman told her.

"Are there any other questions?" Sister Maura asked.

There was silence and shaking of heads.

"Then you can go now, Esperanza. Thanks for going through that ordeal."

As she was walking around the table the Latina woman stopped her for a moment and told her: "*Nuestra Señora te sanará.*"

"*Gracias. Espero que sí.*"

She walked out of Morrissey Hall with mixed feelings about the meeting. Clearly, the black man and the Latina woman were on her side, and the white man with freckles was sympathetic—at least he understood why she hadn't wanted her parents to find out about it. The white woman in glasses hadn't said much, but she had agreed with the Latina woman on the issue of men having doubts about women. The Latino guy hadn't committed himself either way, and the big white girl was the least sympathetic. Did she really think that one girl could have fought off those four guys? Or was something else going on with her?

As she walked across the campus Esperanza counted the probable votes of the committee in the worst case scenario. Three in her favor if she included Sister Maura, who hadn't needed to ask questions. Three undecided, and one against. So the man with freckles was the key to getting a majority vote in her favor.

Wanting to talk with someone about it, she texted Griselda, who replied within five minutes, saying that she was in class now but it was supposed to end at one thirty. They arranged to meet in Griselda's room at quarter of two.

She stopped at the cafeteria and bought four slices of pizza, which she took in a box to the dormitory—the woman at reception made a comment about how good it smelled. Griselda had left the door open for her, and she went in with the pizza, which they ate while they talked, Esperanza at the desk and Griselda on her bed.

"I guess it could have gone worse," she told her friend. "At least they didn't all think I should have fought those guys off."

"Should have or could have?" Griselda asked.

"Is there a difference?"

"There might not be a difference in English, but there is in Spanish. Should have means you had a moral obligation to fight them off, whereas could have means you had the power to fight them off."

"If I didn't have the power to fight them off, then how could I have had a moral obligation to fight them off?"

"I don't know. I guess the guys who invented the difference never were in your position."

"Well, anyway there was a girl on the committee who thought I could have fought them off. She was a big white girl."

"What was her name?"

"They called her Diane."

"She's a student?"

"Yeah. She's the student representative on some committee."

"Didn't they give you a list of the people on the disciplinary committee?"

"Sister Maura emailed me a list of the members, but I didn't pay much attention to it. I didn't know any of the people. I mean, except Sister Maura."

"Do you still have her message?"

"Yeah." She put down the slice of pizza and reached for her smartphone. It took her only a few minutes to find the email. "That girl has an Italian last name, and she's in the accounting program."

"That wouldn't explain it. But you said she was a big girl, so maybe she thought that if she'd been in your position, she could have fought those guys off."

"Maybe. But maybe she was implying that if I'd *wanted* to fight them off, I could have."

"You mean to undermine your claim that they raped you."

"Yeah. I don't know why, but I had the feeling she was on the side of those guys."

"She's white, and they're white."

"Oh, I don't think it was racial. The one who gave me the most support was a black man."

"What's his name?"

She looked at the list. "John Wingate. He's director of student activities."

"I don't know him, but I've heard good things about him."

"But he didn't support me because of the color of my skin. He supported me because he understood what happened."

After a silence Griselda asked: "Do you think those guys attacked you because of the color of your skin?"

"No. They attacked me because I'm a female."

"But what if you'd been a white girl?"

"They would have done the same thing."

"I wonder. You said they called you a spic."

"Yeah, but they could have called the white girl a bitch."

"Maybe they had two reasons for attacking you," Griselda speculated. "Because you're a female and because you're a spic."

"But I don't understand either reason. Why would you want to hurt someone just because she's different from you?"

"I have no idea why. But it happens every day."

"It happens in my neighborhood, but I never thought it would happen on this campus."

"Yeah, it's supposed to be safe here."

"Maybe it's not safe anywhere."

"I learned in my psychology course that being safe is a fundamental human need. But maybe it's an unrealistic need."

"Whatever it is, I don't want it to become my top priority," Esperanza said. "You know the girl who showed me the video? I think it's her top priority to make the world safe for women—by getting rid of all the men."

"Well, that's pretty drastic," Griselda said.

"She wants the guys who raped me to be punished."

"Do *you* want them to be punished?"

"That's what the man with freckles asked me."

"The man with freckles?"

"A faculty member." She looked back at the list. "His name is Myron Ginsberg. He teaches psychology."

"So what did you tell him?"

"I told him I didn't want them to be punished, I only wanted to get back in the good graces of my father."

"Did he understand?"

"I think he did. I know the Latina woman did." Before being prompted she looked back at the list. "Her name is Solana, Sister Solana. I should have known she was a nun."

"*Sólo quieres volver a la buena voluntad de tu padre*," Griselda repeated. "I understand. And I'll pray to Our Lady of Altagracia that it will happen."

Esperanza appeared again before the committee on Friday. She sat at the foot of the table and listened to the instructions from Sister Maura, who had set a lined yellow page in front of her with the numbers one to eight in the left column.

"We've asked eight male students to join us," Sister Maura said. "Each of them will read a passage to you, and if you recognize his voice as one of your assailants, then write 'Yes' opposite his number on the paper in front of you. If you don't recognize his voice, write 'No.' Do you have any questions?"

"No," she said, understanding the purpose of the exercise. But she wasn't sure if she would recognize their voices.

The receptionist brought eight guys into the boardroom and told them to sit in chairs that had been arranged along the wall, about five feet from the table. They weren't horsing around as guys usually did, they weren't all taking this seriously.

"Do you recognize any of these young men?" Sister Maura asked her.

"No. I've never seen any of them before."

The receptionist gave each of the guys a sheet of paper with a number on it, one to eight, and asked them to hold the sheets in front of them so people sitting at the table could see them. She then gave each of them another sheet of paper.

"Number one," Sister Maura said, "please read the passage."

The guy cleared his throat and read: "What you do to the least of my brothers and sisters, you do to me."

Esperanza listened carefully, but she didn't recognize the voice, so she wrote: "No."

The next guy was also "No," but the next one she recognized as the one who said: "You had your turn. It's my turn now."

After another "No" was the guy who said: "Yeah, she asked for it."

The next guy was "No," and the next guy read the passage in a falsetto voice.

"Come on," Sister Maura said. "Read it in your normal voice."

"That *is* my normal voice," the guy insisted.

She noticed that he had a tattoo on his right forearm. It was two lacrosse sticks, forming a diagonal cross. It didn't look like a religious symbol.

"I know your normal voice. You're in one of my courses. So read it in your normal voice."

He finally read the passage in his normal voice, and she recognized him as the leader, the guy who said: "I'm going to do something before we leave her."

The next two guys were "No," and that was it.

"Thank you," Sister Maura said. "You can go now."

The guys got up and shuffled out.

"Could I see that paper?"

She folded it and passed it to Diane, who passed it to the man with freckles.

When the paper reached her, Sister Maura unfolded it and examined it, saying: "She got all three of them."

"That doesn't prove anything," Diane said. "She had three chances in eight of guessing them correctly."

"No, she didn't," the man with freckles said. "The odds of her guessing all three of them correctly are one in fifty-six, so she had less than a two percent chance of guessing them. For me that's significant."

"How did you figure that?"

"This isn't the time for a tutorial in statistics. If you want to schedule one, you can call my office."

"What you just did," Sister Maura told her, "was identify three of the guys who attacked you. We already had their names from the fourth guy, and you verified what he said in his statement. In addition, the police matched the fingerprints of their leader with the prints on beer cans that were left at the scene. So we have no doubt about their identity."

"You went to the police?" she said, alarmed by what that might lead to.

"We didn't take your case to them. We only asked them about the fingerprints."

She sighed in relief, covering her face with her shaky hands.

"Why don't you want the police involved?" Diane asked.

That hit a nerve. She removed her hands from her face and glared at the girl. "If you were raped, would you want it in all the newspapers?"

"It's on the internet."

"Diane, that's enough," Sister Maura said.

"Well, I don't think you're being fair to those guys," Diane said. "And when are we going to hear their side of it?"

"In a few minutes. I asked them to stay."

Diane folded her arms and sat back. "Okay. Let's hear their side of it."

"Do you want me to leave?" Esperanza asked.

"No, I want you to stay."

"Is that fair?" Diane asked.

"Yes, it's fair," John said. "In case you've forgotten, she's the victim. She's not on trial, they are. And if this was a court, she'd have a right to hear what they say about her."

"What about their right to hear what she says about them?"

"They're going to hear it," Sister Maura said. She called the receptionist and asked her to bring the guys in. Again, Jeffrey wasn't among them. After asking them to sit at the table, Sister Maura introduced them as Brandon, Scott, and Kenny.

"What about the fourth guy?" Diane asked.

"He's testifying against them," Maura explained, "so we've separated him from them."

"Are they going to hear what he says about them?"

"Yes, they are. In another meeting."

"I have no problem with this process," the man with freckles said. "Let's proceed."

"Would one of you like to speak for the group?" Sister Maura asked the guys.

"Yeah, I will," Brandon said confidently.

"So tell us what happened."

"Well, we were at a spot where we often go, it's off the path that overlooks the river. We were drinking beer, and this girl came along and asked if she could join us."

"I never did," Esperanza said. "You're lying."

"Let him make his statement," Sister Maura told her, "and then you can contest it."

"So we said she could, and she started drinking with us. In fact, she got drunk and passed out. You can see her in the video, lying unconscious. And when she came to, she took off her clothes and asked to have sex with all of us."

"If that's what happened," the man with freckles said, "how do you explain the fact that she was gagged and blindfolded?"

"She asked us to gag her and blindfold her. She wanted to have rough sex."

"It didn't look like rough sex. It looked like rape."

"It's not rape," Brandon said, "if the girl asks for it. And this girl asked for it."

"She was insatiable," Scott said. "After three of us had sex with her she still wanted more."

"Did the fourth guy have sex with her?" the man with freckles asked.

"No, he couldn't get it up," Brandon snickered.

"Did she ask you to do what you did before you left her?"

"Oh, yeah. She begged me to do it. I thought it was kinky, but I obliged her. I like to make women happy."

"You're full of shit," the black man said looking as if he wanted to kill Brandon.

"John, please," Sister Maura said.

"I'm sorry, sister, but I can't stand it. This young punk actually expects us to believe him?"

"I'm telling the truth," Brandon said as if he was offended.

"You're lying through your teeth," John said.

"I believe him," Diane said, though not convincingly.

"You do? Why? Because he's—"

"Don't say it, John," Sister Maura warned him. "We don't want to taint this process. Esperanza, would you like to contest what he said?"

"Yeah, I would," she said, trying to stay calm. "When you're on that path you can't see the spot where they were drinking, so I couldn't have seen them and asked to join them. And I don't know what he means by 'rough sex.' I was a virgin, and I feel like I still am because I didn't have sex with them. I was raped by them."

"You asked for it," Brandon maintained.

"I didn't ask you to ram into me and bang me. I didn't ask you to tear me apart. And I didn't ask you to pee on me."

"You did. You wanted it."

"Where did you learn what women want?" the Latina woman asked him.

"I learned from experience, so I know what they want."

"You don't know shit," John said.

"John, please," Sister Maura said. "Try to keep your feelings under control."

"I can't keep them under control. He's saying the things men always say to justify their brutality to women."

"I know he is, but we have to hear his side of it."

There was a long silence.

The Latino guy finally asked: "Have you done this kind of thing before?"

"What do you mean?" Brandon asked.

"I mean gang sex."

"Oh, yeah. I've done a lot of it. I'm the first to admit that I can't satisfy a girl by myself, so I have other guys help me."

"And the girls ask for it?"

"They always do. You must know from your own experience—"

The Latino guy cut him off with a sharp gesture. "I don't have any cxpcricncc with that kind of thing. And if you think girls ask for it, there's something seriously wrong with you."

"Do you have anything more to say?" Sister Maura asked Brandon.

He shook his head, looking put down.

"Do you, Esperanza?"

"Yeah, I do," she said, pulling her locket a few inches out from her chest. "I was wearing this locket when they grabbed me. They ripped it from my neck and threw it into the woods. My parents gave it to me for my *quinceañera.* In case you don't know, in our culture a *quinceañera* is a celebration when a girl turns fifteen. I think you have something like that for girls when they turn sixteen. Inside is a picture of Our Lady of Guadalupe."

"I don't see the point of this," Diane said.

"Let her talk," Sister Maura said.

Esperanza opened the locket and showed them the picture. "Our Lady was there, and she can confirm that I told you the truth about what happened. So listen to her."

She closed her eyes and held her breath.

It was a long time before anyone in the room made a sound, but finally Sister Solana said: "*La escuché.* I heard her."

She was sitting in a quiet corner of the library, trying to study but unable to concentrate on the material because of the turmoil in her head, when her phone signaled the arrival of a text message. She assumed it was from Griselda, wanting to know how the meeting had gone, but it was from Sister Solana, who must have gotten her phone number from someone. The message said: "Can you meet me on the patio outside the cafeteria?"

Without thinking she replied: "Yes. When?"

"Whenever you can."

"I can meet you now."

"I'll see you there in a few minutes."

Though she was encouraged by the invitation, she couldn't imagine why Sister Solana wanted to meet with her. She understood enough about the process to know they couldn't talk about the meetings of the disciplinary committee, and she had never taken a course with Sister Solana, so what were they going to talk about?

When she walked out to the patio Sister Solana was waiting for her, and she greeted her with a warm smile, saying: *"Gracias por venir con tan poco aviso."*

"No hay problema," she said, feeling reassured.

"We need some privacy to talk, so let's go to the path that overlooks the river. Is that okay with you?"

"Yeah, it's okay." She followed Sister Solana down the hill to the athletic field, where luckily the lacrosse team wasn't practicing.

"Where are your parents from?" Sister Solana asked as they crossed the athletic field.

"They're from Mexico, the city of Puebla."

"My parents are from the Dominican Republic, the city of Santiago."

That explained why Sister Solana spoke Spanish with the same accent as Griselda. It also explained why she was tall.

"Were you born here?" Sister Solana asked her.

"My younger brother and I were born here, so we were both automatically citizens. But my parents had to go through the process of becoming citizens."

"Have you ever been to Mexico?"

"No. My parents became citizens only a year ago, so we couldn't leave the country before. And now they don't have time to go there."

"I understand. After more than twenty years my parents finally returned for a visit to Santiago. They said they hardly recognized it."

They reached the path and walked along in silence for a while.

Then Sister Solana said: "I love this walk. I come here every morning, except when it's too cold. I always feel peaceful here."

"I know what you mean. I used to feel peaceful here."

"Have you come here since it happened?"

"Only once—to look for my locket."

"I had a similar experience," Sister Solana said quietly, "and I avoided going back to the place where it happened."

"You mean you were raped?"

"I was attacked by a gang of guys, and the only thing that stopped them from raping me was my fiancé, who heard my cries for help and came to my rescue. He stopped them, but before they got away, they killed him."

"Oh, my God. I'm sorry."

"It happened a long time ago."

Again, they walked along in silence, and when they came to the place where those guys had assaulted her, Solana stopped as if she knew it had happened here.

As she gazed down over the boulders Esperanza was overcome by mixed feelings of outrage and shame. For a moment she was stunned, but then she recovered enough to ask: "Why did you bring me here?"

"I want you to know your life didn't end here."

"I know it didn't, but I feel like it did."

"It took me a long time to get over it. The worst thing was, I lost my faith. I could no longer believe in a God who would let such things happen."

"But why *does* God let such things happen?"

"A standard answer to that question is, to test our faith. I used to believe that, but it didn't work for me, and I finally realized that it's not to test our faith, it's to fulfill a plan."

Esperanza thought about this. "So the plan was for you to become a nun?"

"That's right. And the plan wouldn't have been fulfilled if my fiancé and I had gotten married and had children."

"But you would have been a mother."

"I wanted to be a mother," Sister Solana said, turning to gaze across the river. "And I almost did become a mother, but that wasn't God's plan."

"Are you happy being a nun?"

"Yes. I'm very happy."

"Well, I hope you're not suggesting that the plan for me is to become a nun."

Sister Solana laughed heartily. *"Dios mío, no.* I'm only suggesting that there's a plan for you, and that what happened to you here is part of it."

"I don't see how. And anyway I've lost my faith."

"You haven't lost your faith."

"How would you know?"

"I know from the way you showed us your locket and told us about Our Lady of Guadalupe."

"It was only hope, it wasn't faith."

"Would it be faith if the committee makes the decision you're hoping for?"

"I don't know."

"Would you thank God for that decision?"

"I guess I would," Esperanza admitted.

"You'd give God credit for it. So it would be faith, which is the realization of what is hoped for."

"Maybe," Esperanza said with an open mind. "But I still don't see how what happened to me here could be part of a plan."

"I don't either," Sister Solana admitted. "But it probably has to do with the guy who wants a reconciliation."

"If it is, then I don't see how a reconciliation could justify what happened to me."

"It wouldn't justify what happened to you. But it would give you an opportunity to be an instrument of God's mercy."

"Why should I be an instrument of God's mercy?"

"So you can know God. His name is mercy."

Though she didn't understand this, she absorbed it, hoping that someday she would understand it. But it made her wonder if a reconciliation might have more value than she had imagined.

That evening she got off work at ten as usual and she walked home and joined her mother in front of the television. She had already told her mother about the meeting, so there was no need to talk about it. She could sit on the sofa next to her mother and watch a Mexican soap opera, escaping into another world.

Her father got home shortly after the end of the episode, and he slumped in a chair next to the sofa, looking exhausted.

After muting the television her mother asked: "*Estás bien?*"

"Yeah, I'm all right," her father said wearily. "I just haven't been sleeping well."

"None of us have," her mother said.

"How did the meeting go today?" he asked Esperanza.

"It went fine. I had to identify the guys who did it, and then I had to contest their version of what happened. But all except one of the committee believed me."

"*Debe haber sido un varón*," her mother said.

"It wasn't a male. It was a female, a big white girl. She's the student representative on some committee."

"Maybe she was playing politics," her father said.

"I think she has a problem with Latinos."

"She's not the only one."

"But a white man with freckles put her down, and a black man strongly supported me."

"So how do you think they'll rule?"

"I think they'll rule in my favor."

"If they do, what will happen to those guys?"

"They'll be expelled from the college."

"They won't go to prison?"

"It's not a court. It's a college committee."

"Then maybe you should take them to court."

"Now, wait a minute," she told her father. "You said that if they ruled in my favor, you'd be satisfied."

"Well, maybe I won't be," her father said stubbornly.

"You've already put her through hell," her mother said. "Do you have any idea what it was like for her to go before that committee and tell them what those guys did to her?"

"I know it was hard, but they shouldn't get away with it."

"They won't get away with it. They'll be punished by being expelled from college."

"That's not enough for me."

"It's enough for me," Esperanza said, "and I'm the one they did it to."

"We won't gain anything by their going to prison," her mother argued. "And what if the court ruled in their favor?"

"You think it could?" her father said as if he hadn't considered the possibility.

"Those guys are from rich families. They can hire lawyers, they can pay off the judge."

"How do you know they're from rich families?"

"They play a sport that's played only in rich, white suburbs."

"Where did you get that information?"

"From a person at work. There's a nurse on our floor who lives in Hastings, and I asked her about it. Her son wanted to play that sport, but she wouldn't let him. She made him try out for the baseball team."

"Okay, okay," her father said. "If the committee rules in your favor, you don't have to take those guys to court. But they better rule in your favor."

"We'll pray that they do," her mother said.

ELEVEN

JEFFREY WAS FIFTEEN minutes early for the meeting of the committee on Wednesday. He was waiting in the reception area when Brandon, Scott, and Kenny arrived, a few minutes late. They didn't have time to say anything to him before the receptionist led them into the boardroom. Sister Maura asked him to sit at the foot of the table, and she had the other guys sit together on one side of the table, between a black man and a woman with glasses.

Sister Maura introduced the members of the committee to him—evidently the other three guys had already met with the committee—and then she asked him to read his statement, which he had brought with him. While he read he kept his eyes on the paper, not wanting to engage with the members of the committee because he was so ashamed of what he had done. And he read slowly, wanting to make it clear what had happened.

"Thank you, Jeffrey," Sister Maura said when he was finished. "Do the committee members have any questions?"

"I have a question," the man with freckles said. "You said you pinned Esperanza's arms while the other guys raped her. Did you know what you were doing was wrong?"

"Oh, yeah. I knew it was wrong."

"Then why did you do it?"

"I don't know. I did what Brandon asked me to do."

"I didn't ask you to pin her arms," Brandon said.

"Let them finish," Sister Maura said.

"Did you say anything to the other guys while they were raping her?" the man with freckles continued.

"Yeah. I remember saying that she was a virgin—because there was blood."

"There wasn't any blood," Brandon said dismissively.

"You'll have a chance to speak," Sister Maura told him. "Please let them finish."

"Did you say anything else to them?"

"Yeah, when Brandon started peeing on her, I said he shouldn't do that."

"You waited until *then* to say they shouldn't do what they were doing to her?"

"Yeah," he admitted. "I saw what they were doing to her, but I didn't try to stop them. I went along with them."

"What made you go along with them?"

"I don't know. I guess because they were my teammates."

The man with freckles nodded as if he understood. "You wanted to build your relationship with them?"

"Yeah. I wanted to be one of them."

"You wanted to be one of them?" the black man asked with outrage. "If they'd decided to kill that girl, would you have wanted to be one of them?"

"No, I wouldn't have."

"Are you sure?"

"I'm sure."

"So it's okay to rape a girl, but it's not okay to kill her?"

"It's not okay to rape a girl," he said with contrition. "It's a mortal sin, it's a major felony."

"Well, I'm glad you understand that."

"I have a question," the big girl said. "Did the girl consent to having sex with those guys?"

"Of course she didn't. She was gagged and blindfolded and held down. She couldn't see us, she couldn't scream, and she couldn't move."

"Did she ask to be gagged and blindfolded and held down?"

"Are you kidding?" He wondered where on earth this girl was coming from.

"Please answer her question," Sister Maura told him.

"No, she didn't ask to be gagged and blindfolded and held down. She was unconscious when they did that to her."

"You said 'they' but didn't you help them?"

"I admitted what I did. I pinned her arms while the other guys raped her."

"Was she unconscious because she passed out from drinking too much beer?"

"She didn't drink any beer with us. As I said in my statement, she was walking along the path alone when Brandon grabbed her from behind and got her in a chokehold."

"Did you see him do that?"

"I saw him carry her down from the path over his shoulder."

"I have a question," the Latina woman said after a silence. "Did you see a silver locket on a chain around Esperanza's neck?"

"I don't remember seeing it at the time," he said, "but when I went back to the spot the next morning I spotted it lying in the woods."

"Why did you go back there?"

"I wanted to know if it really happened."

"You didn't believe it?"

"I guess I didn't. I mean, I didn't want to believe it. But when I went back there and saw the locket, I believed it."

"So you found the locket. What did you do with it?"

"I picked it up and took it with me. I thought of leaving it there for her, but I was afraid that someone else would pick it up and then she wouldn't get it back."

"Did you try to give it to her?"

"Yeah, I did. But she wouldn't take it from me. So I asked Sister Maura to give it to her."

"He did," Sister Maura said, "and I gave it to her."

"I have another question," the Latina woman said, looking at him closely. "Why did you want Esperanza to have the locket?"

"I knew it was something of value to her. Inside was a picture of Our Lady of Guadalupe."

"How did you know it was Our Lady of Guadalupe?"

"I checked the picture on the internet."

"It sounds like you wanted to make amends."

"I did, and I do. But I can never do enough to atone for what I did to her."

"I have no further questions," the Latina woman said softly.

"I have a comment," the Latino guy said. "I grew up in a rough neighborhood in south Yonkers, where there were gangs. When I was a kid I joined a gang, and whatever they did, I went along with them because I wanted to be one of them. So I can understand why you went along with them. We did some bad things, but we never raped anyone or killed anyone."

"We didn't rape anyone," Brandon said.

"What *did* you do?" the man with freckles asked.

"We only did what that girl asked us to do. And Jeffrey told her where she could find us."

"I did not," Jeffrey objected.

"Let Brandon speak," Sister Maura said.

"He knew she was a hot little number," Brandon said, "so he asked her to join us."

"I thought *she* asked to join you," the man with freckles said.

"She asked to join us through Jeffrey. She heard we were studs, and she wanted to have sex with us."

"So she and Jeffrey arranged the whole thing?"

"Yeah. If you think about it, they used us."

"I'm thinking about it. So you were victims of a conspiracy between Jeffrey and Esperanza?"

"Yeah, we were," Brandon said.

"Well, let me ask you, what could they gain by bringing false charges against you?"

"They could gain money. They know our parents have a lot of money, and they could blackmail us."

"That makes sense," the big girl said, nodding.

"It doesn't make any sense at all," the black man said. "Can you imagine this guy and that girl concocting such a scheme?"

"He made the video," Brandon said, "so he could use it to blackmail us."

"How could he have made the video if he was in it?"

"He wasn't in it."

"He was in every scene, pinning her arms."

"That wasn't him, it was me."

The black man smiled and turned to Sister Maura. "If you think it's necessary, we could watch the video again, and we could have these guys take down their pants so we can compare their naked butts to the naked butts of the guys in the video."

"I don't think it's necessary," Sister Maura said. "I think we've heard enough."

"This process isn't fair," Brandon said. "You didn't give us a chance to tell our side of it."

"We gave you a chance, and all you did was blame Jeffrey and Esperanza. You took no responsibility for what happened."

"Why should we take responsibility for something that wasn't our fault?"

"We're not asking you to do that," the man with freckles said. "We're asking you to tell us the truth."

"We told you the truth."

"Well, I can only speak for myself, but I don't believe you told us the truth. I believe you lied about everything."

"You know," Brandon said with a look of disdain. "My father's a lawyer, and when he hears how you treated me, you'll be sorry."

"When he hears how you treated that girl," the black man said, "*you'll* be sorry."

"He won't believe it."

"Maybe he won't. And you know what? I really don't care if he believes it."

"John, please," Sister Maura said.

The black man clamped his mouth shut.

"Are there any more questions?"

No one said a word.

"Then you can go," Sister Maura told the four guys.

Jeffrey let the other guys go first, and then he followed them.

But they were waiting for him outside.

"You piece of shit," Brandon said. "You're going to get our asses kicked out of here."

"I hope so. You don't belong here."

"Who the hell are you to say we don't belong here?"

"It's only my opinion," Jeffrey said. "The committee will decide if you belong here."

"We want you to retract your statement."

"I'm not going to retract it."

"You know, we could hurt you," Brandon said, "and they'd never know who did it."

"I think they'd guess, so you're not in a good position to threaten me. Anyway, I don't care if you kill me."

"You don't? Why not?"

"Because I don't know how I'm going to live with myself after what I did to that poor girl."

"He doesn't know how he's going to live with himself," Brandon said mockingly. "What a fucking pussy."

"I have a lot of things to do," he told them, starting to walk around them.

"Yeah, one thing is to retract your statement."

"I'm not going to. So get out of my way."

Brandon pushed him, and he reacted by swinging a fist into Brandon's face. It evidently surprised Brandon, who fell backward onto the sidewalk with blood gushing from his nose. Seeing their leader knocked down, the other guys didn't make a move.

And Jeffrey was free to walk away.

In a tumult of feelings he went to his room and left his backpack and then went out and left the campus. As he walked south on Broadway he thought about the meeting, and he was sure that all four of them would be expelled. But for him that wasn't enough of a punishment, and it left him wondering what he could do to atone for his sin.

Approaching St. Brigid he saw Father Paul talking with a woman in front of the church. As usual he had a cigarette in his left hand, which he held at a distance from the woman.

As Jeffrey got closer to them he saw that the woman was his mother's age, or maybe even older. She had dark hair with streaks of gray and luminous skin.

"Hey, Jeffrey," Father Paul said, welcoming him. "This is Sara."

The woman extended a hand, which he promptly shook.

"Sara lives in the neighborhood. She teaches at our school. For how long?"

"Twenty-four years," the woman said happily.

"Jeffrey's a student at St. Catherine. He started there this fall."

"That's great. How do you like it?"

"I like it fine," he said, conscious of the fact that by next week he would be expelled.

"Well, I have to go and shop for food," the woman said. "It was nice meeting you, Jeffrey. And it's always nice talking with you, father."

When she was beyond hearing distance Father Paul said: "She's a good teacher and a good woman. She was just telling me that her daughter was accepted into the graduate program for social work at Fordham University."

"How old is her daughter?" he asked, not knowing what else to say.

"She's twenty-two. I baptized her," the priest added as if he couldn't believe that so much time had passed.

He waited for Father Paul to finish his cigarette, and then he followed him into the church, where they sat down in their usual places.

He began by saying: "I met with the committee today."

"How did it go?" Father Paul asked.

"It didn't go well. I mean, they asked some tough questions."

"Like what?"

"Like why did I go along with those guys, and why didn't I try to stop them?"

"Those are the questions you've been asking yourself all along. Did you come up with any answers?"

"No, I didn't," Jeffrey said. "But a member of the committee, a Latino guy, talked about his own experience in going along with other guys because he wanted to be one of them. And I think that's the best explanation."

"I think it is."

"But it's only an explanation, it's not an excuse."

"No, it's not an excuse."

"I think we're all going to be expelled, but I feel like I deserve a much worse punishment. And I'm looking for something I can do to atone for my sin."

"Beyond the usual ten Hail Marys."

"Yeah. I understand that when they find you guilty in a court, instead of sending you to prison they can make you do community service."

"They can do that for misdemeanors."

"What about felonies?"

"I don't know. But the case won't go to court, will it?"

"It won't if the committee rules in Esperanza's favor, and based on what I heard today, I think it will."

"Then the legal classification of your crime has no meaning for this purpose."

"I guess it doesn't. So what do you think?"

"I think it would be appropriate for you to do community service. If they expel you, will you go home to Poughkeepsie?"

"I could. But if I'm at home my parents will see me every day, and they'll be reminded of what I did."

"They'll forgive you," Father Paul said.

"I guess they will. I mean, they're my parents. They have to forgive anything I do."

"They don't have to, so don't take it for granted."

"I won't. But their forgiveness wouldn't mean as much as Esperanza's forgiveness."

"No, it wouldn't."

"So I want to do something that would give her a reason to forgive me."

"You mean like doing service for *her* community?"

"Yeah. From what I saw when I went to her neighborhood, they need a lot of help there."

"They certainly do," Father Paul said. "In fact, our church is involved in helping them."

"It is? Then tell me how I could get involved."

Father Paul rubbed his chin, thinking. "Your parents have a restaurant, and you work at a restaurant, so you know about food. And that would make you useful for the food pantry and the soup kitchen at San Pedro."

"San Pedro?" He wondered if it was in a foreign country.

"It's the church in Esperanza's neighborhood. It does a lot for her community, and our church supports its programs. So you could get involved in those programs."

"That sounds perfect. How do I start?"

"Well, first you need a place to live." Father Paul paused. "I have an empty room in the rectory. We used to have three priests here, but we're down to two, and one of them is temporary, so that room is available. But it's only a room."

"I live in a room in the dormitory, so I'm used to not having much space."

"You could have it free—in return for doing odd jobs."

"I'll do whatever you need done."

"Then we have a deal. I'll have the room cleaned so it'll be ready for you next week. And if you're available later today, I'll take you down to San Pedro and introduce you to the guy who runs its food programs."

"I'm available. I was going to study, but there isn't any point in doing that now."

"There evidently isn't," the priest said. "So come back at four."

When he came back there was a ten-year-old black car in front of the church, and Father Paul was waiting for him. They drove south on Broadway and down the hill and toward the river and then south again and finally to an intersection where Father Paul did a U-turn and then turned right into a parking lot.

They got out of the car, and Father Paul led him to a back door, which he opened as if he knew his way around. There was a small entrance hall and then a room that was bigger than most of the classrooms at the college. Its floor was mostly covered with boxes that might have been organized but exactly how wasn't apparent.

A man was standing beside a desk with two teenage Latino boys who were probably supposed to be helping him but were engrossed in their smartphones.

"Hey, Arlen," Father Paul said, heading toward the man. "I have a new assistant for you."

Arlen smiled, displaying front teeth with a space between them. He was probably about the same age as Father Paul, with gray hair and a gray beard and playful blue eyes.

"This is Jeffrey," Father Paul said, introducing him. "He's a student at St. Catherine, but he's planning to take a year off from college to do community service."

"I'm glad to meet you," Arlen said, shaking his head. "I wish I'd done that at your age. I might have gone in a better direction."

"Arlen was a corporate executive," Father Paul said, "until he realized that he could do better things for society."

"When can you start?" Arlen asked him.

"When do you need me?"

"I need you right away. Thanksgiving is next week, and that's an especially busy time for us."

"I was planning to spend Thanksgiving with my family, but—"

"I don't need you on Thanksgiving Day. I need you to help me get ready for it."

"Then I could start tomorrow," Jeffrey said. "What time?"

"Can you get here by nine in the morning? You can go around with me in the van and pick up donations of food."

"Sure. I'll see you tomorrow."

"Just come in the back door and you'll find me here."

As they walked back to the car Jeffrey said: "That's the shortest job interview I ever had, except the one I had with my father."

"We go back a long way."

"Well, thanks for giving me a cover."

"If I'd told him the truth about why you're leaving college, he still would have hired you. He works a lot with troubled kids."

"Am I a troubled kid?"

"Yeah, you are," Father Paul said. "Though I've seen worse."

For the next several days he worked to help Arlen get ready for Thanksgiving. They went around in a white van to churches, food stores, and other places where donated food was collected. Arlen knew the pastors, store managers, and site directors of all the places, and he always took the time to chat with them. He had a bad back, so Jeffrey did the heavy lifting.

He planned to keep his job at the restaurant in Hastings. With that job and a free place to live, he could support himself and have the rest of his time available to help Arlen and do odd jobs at St. Brigid. He arranged with Arlen to let him leave by four on Friday and Saturday so on those days he could work dinner at the restaurant, catching a train to Hastings from the Ludlow station. Arlen took Sunday off, so on that day Jeffrey could work both brunch and dinner.

On Sunday he went to the ten o'clock mass at San Pedro, which Arlen had told him was in Spanish. He sat in a pew near the back of the church, on the left aisle. He saw Esperanza with her family in a pew near the front, and he prayed for her.

He was able to follow the mass in Spanish, more or less, and when the time came for Communion he remained seated, feeling unworthy to receive the sacrament. He watched Esperanza slowly going up the center aisle with her father and her mother and her brother. He hoped he would have a chance to talk with her when the mass was ended.

Since he was sitting at a side aisle, he was able to get out of the church ahead of everyone except for the people way in the back, and he was standing on the sidewalk when Esperanza emerged with her family.

Her father spotted him and gave him a look that could have killed, but in front of the church he had to control himself. He put an arm around his daughter to guide her away.

"Can we talk for a minute?" Jeffrey asked her. There wasn't a better time to ask her since she had just come out of church after saying a prayer that included forgiving those who had trespassed against her.

"*Está bien, papá,*" she told her father, freeing herself from his arm.

"*Sólo por un minuto,*" her father said grudgingly.

She said something in Spanish that must have asked her family not to wait for her because they left her and started walking.

He headed away from the crowd in front of the church toward the other side of the entrance to the parking lot, and she went along with him. When they reached a place where they could talk in private, they stopped.

"How did your meeting go?" she asked.

"It didn't go well," he said, repeating what he had said to Father Paul. "They asked me why I went along those guys."

She was silent, listening.

"I said I went along with them because I wanted to be one of them. And that's the truth, the pathetic truth."

"You didn't go along with them all the way."

"I went along with them too far."

Again she was silent, and then she said: "You found my locket and returned it to me."

"That doesn't make amends for what I did to you."

"It doesn't, but it was a good thing."

"Well, whether or not they expel me, I'm leaving college and I'm going to do community service. In fact, I'm working here in your neighborhood."

"Doing what?" she asked, looking surprised.

"Helping Arlen with the food pantry."

"That's also a good thing."

"But I don't know if I can do enough good things in my whole lifetime to make amends for what I did. And I don't know if I can ever forgive myself."

"To be honest," she said, "I don't know if I can ever forgive you. When I think about how you pinned my arms so that those guys could rape me, I want to make you pay for what you did. But when I think about how you returned my locket to me, I want to forgive you. So if you keep doing good things, eventually maybe I will forgive you."

"Thanks," he said, extending his hands with the palms up as some people did when they said the Lord's Prayer. "You've given me hope."

Gingerly, and only for a moment, she touched the palms of his hands with hers.

TWELVE

BECAUSE OF THE break for Thanksgiving, which began on Wednesday, the committee was scheduled to meet at noon on Monday, and Maura hoped that at this meeting they would make a decision on the case. For Esperanza's sake, she wanted the decision to be unanimous since that should leave no doubt in the mind of her father, but she was concerned about Diane, who from the beginning seemed to take the side of the guys. So she asked Diane to meet with her alone at eleven that morning.

Diane was right on time, carrying a briefcase instead of a backpack like other students. She was an honors student in her last year of the public accounting program, and she already had a presence that would serve her well in the workplace.

"Thanks for coming early," Maura said.

"No problem," Diane said, sitting in the chair next to the desk.

"I hear you're doing a very good job on the academic affairs committee."

"I'm doing my best. We have a lot of issues to deal with."

Getting to the point, Maura said: "I wanted to talk about our gang rape case."

"What about it?" Diane asked uneasily.

"Do you have any doubts about what happened?"

"I have doubts about the process. I think some members of the committee are biased against those guys."

"Why would they be biased?"

"Because they're lacrosse players."

"I don't understand."

"Whenever a girl says she's been gang raped on a college campus," Diane said earnestly, "it's always the lacrosse players."

"Can you give me an example?"

"Yeah, I can. The case at Duke University."

"That's only one case, and it was settled in favor of the players."

"I'm sure there are other cases." Diane paused, evidently trying to think of one, and then she blurted out: "My boyfriend plays lacrosse at another college, and he says those guys didn't get a fair hearing."

"He does? How does he know about it?"

Diane put her hand to her mouth as if she had said something she shouldn't have.

"Did you discuss the case with him?"

"I mentioned it to him."

"In our first meeting," Maura said, "I reminded you that what goes on at this committee is strictly confidential. I even specifically said that you can't tell your boyfriend."

"I know you did. I'm sorry."

"Since you broke a fundamental rule of our process, I could remove you from the committee."

Diane hung her head and said nothing in her defense.

"But since that wouldn't look good on your record, I'll let you continue serving on the committee as long as you agree to base your decision on the evidence that has been presented and not on what your boyfriend says."

"I agree," Diane said, raising her head.

"You're planning to be an accountant, right?"

"I am. I mean, if I can pass the licensing exam."

"You'll pass that exam. So let me ask you," Maura said, taking advantage of a learning opportunity, "if you were dealing with an accounting issue, would you base your decision on the records or on what your client said?"

"I'd base my decision on the records."

"Good. You'll make a fine accountant."

When all the members of the committee were assembled at the table in the boardroom, Maura began by asking them if they were ready to make a decision. They all raised their hands, including Diane.

"Okay. We have to make two decisions. One, did those guys rape Esperanza? And two, if they did, then how should they be punished?"

"Can you give us a definition of rape?" Myron asked.

"Yes, I can give you a working definition. Since we're not a court, we don't need a legal definition."

"I doubt if we could understand a legal definition."

"Rape," Maura suggested, "is to have sex with another person without their consent."

"You mean when the parties are of legal age."

"Yes, of course. This isn't about statutory rape."

"In the video we saw acts of sexual intercourse, so could you modify your definition by replacing the word 'sex' with the phrase 'sexual intercourse'?"

"I don't have a problem with that. Does everyone agree to this definition?"

They all murmured or signaled assent.

"Okay. We're going to have two ballots. On the first ballot simply write 'Yes' if you believe that those guys raped Esperanza, and 'No' if you believe they didn't. Is that clear?" It evidently was. "Now, before we vote, do you have any comments?"

"I have a comment," John said. "Since the key concept in your definition is 'consent,' then I think we should make our decisions on the basis of whether we believe the girl consented to what they did to her. And while we've heard claims that she consented, we haven't seen any evidence that she did. In fact, we've seen graphic evidence that sexual intercourse was forced upon her."

"That's a good point," Francesca said. "We've also heard from one of the guys that it was forced upon her."

"Any other comments?" Maura asked.

There weren't any, so she passed out the ballots.

After folding her own, she glanced at Diane, whose hand was still poised over her ballot. Maura was confident that the girl would do what she had agreed to, but it was still possible that she truly believed that those guys hadn't raped Esperanza.

When she had all the ballots Maura started opening them, one at a time, and reading what they said: "Yes…yes…yes...yes."

The members of the committee were silent.

There were only three ballots left, and she couldn't tell whose they were.

"Yes…yes…and yes," she said. "It's unanimous."

She couldn't help glancing at Diane, whose eyes revealed a clear conscience.

"Now we have to decide how they should be punished."

"What are the options?" Myron asked.

"We can expel them from the college, or we can suspend them for one year. That's the normal period of suspension," Maura added.

"For this purpose, I think we should consider Jeffrey separately from the other three guys."

"What do the rest of you think?"

"I think he committed a lesser offense," Solana said. "And he shows remorse for what he did. The other guys don't show any remorse."

"Yeah, they act like it's a joke," John said.

"Do you want to decide on the punishment for the three of them together?"

"I think we should," Myron said.

"Juan, you haven't said anything. Do you agree?"

"Yeah, I agree," Juan said. "The other three guys should all get the same punishment."

Maura handed out the ballots, saying: "On this ballot write 'Expel' if you think they should be expelled from the college, and write 'Suspend' if you think they should be suspended."

When she counted the ballots it was unanimous that they should be expelled.

They went through the same process for Jeffrey, and it was unanimous that he should be suspended.

"How do we inform them of our decisions?" Myron asked.

"We'll tell them in person, and then the president will put it in writing."

"I have an issue," John said. "I think the punishment for the three guys should include a mandate to take that damned video off the internet."

"Is it possible to take it off the internet?"

"If you can put it up, you can take it down."

"What do the rest of you think?"

"I think it's a good idea," Francesca said. "As long as people can watch that video, the girl will feel exposed."

"Exposed and humiliated," John said.

"So how can we make them take the video off the internet?"

"We can threaten to sue them," Myron said.

"The girl wouldn't have to sue them?"

"No. The college could also be injured by that video. If people find out where it was made, our reputation will be damaged."

"I like that approach," John said.

"I do too," Solana said. "It doesn't require Esperanza to do anything further."

"Okay," Maura said. "We'll break for an hour, which should give us time to round up the guys, and then we'll reconvene."

After checking his watch Myron said: "So we'll reconvene at two thirty?"

"Yes, at two thirty."

As they filed out of the boardroom she gave Diane a pat on the shoulder, ignoring the rule against touching students.

Then she went to the president's office to inform him of their decision. Santiago had just returned from having lunch with the mayor of Yonkers, and he was in a good mood, until he heard the committee's decision.

"I hope this doesn't make the news," he said glumly.

"It shouldn't," she said, conscious of the leak to Diane's boyfriend. "It's not a legal matter, it's a college matter, so it really shouldn't be public knowledge."

"Well, if it gets out, we'll deal with it. I know that with you as head of the committee, we've done the right thing."

"We've summoned the guys to appear before us an hour from now to hear our decision."

"The timing is good. They would have left on Wednesday for the break." He paused and then asked: "How is the girl doing?"

"I haven't yet told her about our decision. I have to tell the guys first. But it should help her with her father."

"You mean make her father believe it wasn't her fault?"

"Yeah, that's why I wanted a unanimous decision." She decided not to tell the president what she had done to ensure a unanimous decision.

After a pause Santiago said: "I watched the video, and it made me sick."

"We're going to make them take it off the internet. I assume it's all right if we threaten to sue them on behalf of the college."

"You can threaten to draw and quarter them."

"We shouldn't have to go that far."

"My heart goes out to that poor girl," Santiago said, speaking as the father of three daughters.

"We're going to help her deal with it," Maura said, intending to enlist Solana in her mission to bring about a reconciliation.

At two thirty she was seated at the head of the table with all the members present except Francesca, who finally arrived five minutes late with the explanation that she had been resolving a technical issue in financial aid.

When they were ready she asked the receptionist to bring in Brandon, Scott, and Kenny. She instructed them to sit on the left side of the table, where they had sat before.

"We made a decision," Maura said, getting right to the point. "We found that you raped Esperanza Vargas."

"We didn't rape her," Brandon said.

"And we decided to expel you from the college."

"Does that mean we can't come back?"

"It means you can never come back. You don't belong here."

Brandon glared at her, saying: "You're going to hear from my father."

"I hope I do. I'll get him to watch that video. And speaking of the video, you have to take it off the internet."

"What if we don't?"

"The college will sue you, and your parents won't be happy paying all the legal bills."

"You don't have any basis for suing us."

"Yes, we do," Myron said. "Our reputation could be damaged by that video."

There was a long silence.

"When do we have to leave?" Scott asked.

"We want you to leave as soon as possible," Maura said, "but you have until Wednesday."

"Do you have cars?" John asked.

"Yeah, we all have cars," Kenny said.

"Then you can leave today. Your parents don't have to come and get you."

"Are you going to tell our parents about it?" Scott asked.

"Your parents will get a letter from the president," Maura said. "But you have a chance to tell them before they get the letter."

"What about the guy who ratted on us?" Brandon asked after a silence.

"That's no concern of yours. We'll deal with him."

"Are you going to expel him?"

"We're going to suspend him for one year."

"That's not fair," Kenny said. "He's as guilty as we are."

"We're not guilty of anything," Brandon insisted, giving Kenny a malignant look.

"He *is* as guilty as you are," Solana said. "But he shows remorse for what he did, whereas none of you shows any remorse."

"Oh, don't give me that Catholic shit."

"This is a Catholic college," Maura reminded him. "And if you don't respect our values, you shouldn't be here."

Brandon only glowered at her.

"You're dismissed," John told them as if he couldn't wait to get them out of his sight. "You should leave today."

The guys sauntered out of the room without a further comment.

Next they dealt with Jeffrey, who trudged into the room quietly and sat alone on the left side of the table, looking like an utterly lost soul.

"We made a decision," Maura told him. "We found that Esperanza was raped, but because you've shown remorse for what you did to her we decided not to expel you, we decided to suspend you for one year."

"That's not enough," he said.

"It's enough for the college. I know you're being punished in other ways, and I know you're trying to make amends."

He nodded. "Okay. I'll get my things out of the dormitory."

"Will your parents come and get you?" John asked him.

"No, I have someone to help me move. But my parents know what I did to Esperanza. I told them last Thursday. And they were expecting me to be expelled. So I guess they'll be relieved by your decision."

"We'll talk later," Maura told him, not wanting to involve the whole committee in her mission. "You can go now."

When he had gone she thanked the committee and wished them all a happy Thanksgiving. She lingered in the boardroom long enough to send a text message to Esperanza, saying: "The committee ruled unanimously in your favor. You can tell your father."

She was at her desk, reviewing a student paper that was horribly written when the lacrosse coach appeared in her doorway. He was a big guy who must have played the sport himself. They didn't have much of a relationship since he knew she had opposed bringing lacrosse to St. Catherine, and she had attended only one game, whereas she regularly attended games of the soccer, volleyball, basketball, and baseball teams.

"I just heard what you did to my team," he said, sounding very angry.

"I didn't do anything to your team," she said calmly.

"According to Brandon, you kicked out three of my top players."

"The disciplinary committee kicked them out, and it was a unanimous decision."

"Why did the committee kick them out?" the coach asked, folding his arms and leaning against a door jamb.

"He didn't tell you why?"

"No. He said he couldn't tell me."

"Well, I can't tell you. It's confidential."

"He said you kicked them out for good. Is that true?"

"Yes, it's true. They can't come back here."

"To kick them out of college for good, you must believe they did something bad."

"We *know* they did something bad. We have plenty of evidence."

"So how am I going to field a team this spring?"

"I don't know. I guess you could recruit more players."

"It's too late to recruit them for this year."

"I'm sorry," she said. "But next time try to recruit guys who have moral values."

The coach frowned. "You really don't like lacrosse, do you."

"I like it fine, but not at this college. It's not played in the neighborhoods where our students come from."

"Then you should get students from better neighborhoods."

"That's not our mission. Our mission is to offer a quality private education to students who couldn't otherwise afford it."

"You mean to poor people?"

"Yeah, to poor people. Most of our students are below or around the poverty line."

"But if you recruited rich students you could get more money from their families."

"There are more than enough colleges for rich people."

The coach sighed, shifting his weight. "You could at least give me a hint about what those guys did to get kicked out."

"I can only tell you that if I were you, I wouldn't *want* them on my team."

"It was that bad?"

"It was that bad. So forget about them."

Not long after the coach left her office, Esperanza appeared in the doorway, making Maura wonder if the receptionist had already left for the day.

"I got your message," the girl said. "I just came to make sure I understood it."

"Please sit down," Maura told her. "The committee ruled unanimously that those guys raped you, which means they had sexual intercourse with you without your consent."

"Without my consent. That means I didn't let them do it."

"That's right. You didn't encourage them, you didn't entice them, you didn't do anything to give them the idea that you wanted it."

"Then my father will believe it wasn't my fault."

"If he doesn't, let me know, and I'll deal with him. But I'm sure he will. Just tell him the decision was unanimous."

Esperanza paused, and then she asked: "What's going to happen to those guys?"

"It's already happened. They've been expelled."

"Does that mean they can't come back?"

"They can't ever come back."

"What about Jeffrey?"

"He's been suspended for one year."

Esperanza nodded as if she thought that this was fair. "You know, he came to my church last Sunday for the mass in Spanish. And he was waiting for me outside."

"How did your father react to him?"

"My father wasn't happy to see him, but I managed to get him away from my family and talk with him. He said he was doing community service, working for the food pantry of my church. And I know what he's doing. He's trying to make amends for what he did to me, and he wants me to forgive him."

"What did you tell him?"

"I was honest with him. I told him I didn't know if I could ever forgive him."

"You haven't had much time," Maura said. "It happened only a little more than six weeks ago, and your wounds are still a long way from being healed."

"You know what we say in church about how a word can heal our souls? Well, I don't believe that. It takes more than a word."

"It takes a lot of human words, and a lot of human actions. But in church we mean a word from God."

"So why doesn't God say that word and heal my soul?"

"That's a good question, and I don't know the answer. But maybe somehow he's using Jeffrey for that purpose."

"Well, I finally told Jeffrey that if he kept doing good things, eventually maybe I would forgive him."

"What did he say?"

"He said it gave him hope."

"That's what your name means."

"Yeah. The name was my mother's idea. I was her first baby, and she wanted a name that told the world how she felt about me."

"I'm sure she still feels that way about you."

"For a while after it happened, I was afraid she didn't. But now I know she does. And I'm hoping my father will still feel that I'm his treasure, his gift from God."

"Just tell him the decision was unanimous," Maura said again.

When the girl got up to go, Maura got up too, and she broke the rule for the second time that day. She put her arms around Esperanza and hugged her. And the girl responded, making her feel that she hadn't missed much by not having her own children.

She was clearing the papers off her desk, preparing to leave, when Jeffrey appeared in her doorway. By now she was convinced that the receptionist had left for the day, but she didn't mind. She was glad to see Jeffrey.

"You said we'd talk later," he said hesitantly.

"Come in and sit down," she told him.

He sat where Esperanza had been sitting only about twenty minutes ago.

"I'm ready to move out of the dormitory. Father Paul has a room for me in the rectory of St. Brigid, so I'm going to stay there for a while."

"How will you get your things to the rectory?"

"Father Paul's bringing his car to help me."

Silently she thanked Paul. "Did he get you the job with the food pantry at San Pedro?"

"Yeah. How do you know about that?"

"Esperanza told me."

"She told you?" he said with a look of wonder in his eyes.

"Yes, she told me how you went to her church yesterday for the mass in Spanish and waited outside for her."

"Do you think she understands what I'm doing?"

"I think she does. But you have to give her time. As my colleagues in psychology would put it, she had an extremely traumatic experience."

"I can only imagine how she feels."

"Well, keep trying to imagine how she feels, and maybe someday you'll reach her."

"You know," he said after a pause, "she told me that if I keep doing good things, eventually maybe she would forgive me."

"How did that make you feel?"

"It gave me hope."

"Well, that's all she can give you now. She has to be healed before she can give you anything more."

"Do you think she ever will be healed?"

"I don't know. What happened to her was horrible. But people recover from all kinds of things, so eventually maybe she will be healed."

"If she forgives me, will that mean she *has* been healed?"

Maura stopped to think for a moment. "Forgiving you is part of the healing process. So I shouldn't have said she has to be healed before she can give you anything more. I should have said she has to forgive you before she can be healed."

"You mean if I do things that help her to forgive me, I can help her to be healed?"

"Yes, that's what I mean."

He nodded thoughtfully. "I understand."

Before he left her office she broke the rule for the third time that day.

That evening, in the privacy of her room, she brought Solana up to date on her conversations since the committee meeting. Solana listened without comment until she got to the issue of forgiveness.

"You know," Solana said, "I still haven't forgiven the guys who killed Rafael."

"Have you prayed for them?"

"No. Does that make me a bad nun?"

"It makes you human. And I have to admit, I haven't prayed for the guys who raped Esperanza."

"They acted like they were entitled to rape her."

"I had the same feeling."

"The girl wasn't white, so they could do whatever they wanted to her and get away with it."

"I wonder where they got that idea."

"I don't know. I guess from their parents."

"It must have been their parents. That's where kids get most of their ideas."

"But I don't think Jeffrey was raised that way."

"No, I don't think he was."

"So why did he go along with them?"

"I think Juan had the best explanation. Jeffrey wanted to be one of them."

"God help him. Well, at least there's hope for him."

"You don't believe there's hope for the other three guys?"

Solana sighed. "I'm supposed to believe that, but I don't know. I only know we can't help all of them, so let's focus on the two people we have the best chance of helping."

"I'm glad you didn't say 'saving'."

"I almost did say that, but they have to save themselves—with our help and God's help."

After thinking for a moment Maura said: "You can be a good mentor for Esperanza. I mean, not only because you're Latina but also because you had an experience like hers and you had to deal with the issue of forgiveness."

"I'm still dealing with it."

"Then you understand that she'll need time."

"I wasn't raped," Solana said. "They were going to rape me but Rafael stopped them. So I don't know what it's like to be raped."

"You know what it's like to be a victim of male violence."

"Yeah, I do. And I can imagine what would have happened if Rafael hadn't stopped them."

"So you can help her. We can help her together."

"What about Jeffrey?"

"Paul is helping him. I mean, I'll continue trying to help him, but Paul can do more for him."

"Okay. Well, I feel our committee did the right thing."

"I feel we did. And I'm glad it was unanimous."

"You think her father will be satisfied?"

"I don't know her father," Maura said, "but Esperanza thinks he'll be satisfied."

After reflecting, Solana said: "I wondered if it would be unanimous, the way Diane took the side of the guys."

"Between you and me, I talked with her before the committee met today. I found out that she was being influenced by her boyfriend."

"She talked with him about it?"

"Yeah, she did."

"You could have removed her from the committee."

"I could have, but I gave her a chance to make a decision based on the evidence, not on what her boyfriend told her."

"Well, that was better than removing her from the committee. The process wasn't tainted by what she did."

"It wasn't tainted, or at least not much. So it shouldn't be questioned."

"Who would question it?"

"The parents of those guys. You heard what Brandon said about his father. So I wouldn't be surprised if the president calls me tomorrow morning."

He called her at nine, without the help of an intermediary, and asked if she could come to his office right away. She was there in less than ten minutes.

"I got a call from Brandon's father," he told her after the preliminaries, during which she accepted his offer of coffee. "He lives on Long Island, but he was in Yonkers when he called, so he should be here any minute."

"Did he tell you what he wants?"

"No. But I know what he wants. He wants us to change our decision to expel his son."

"Well, I'm willing to listen to his arguments, but unless he has something other than the fact that Brandon is his son, I see no reason to change our decision."

"I don't either. I was just telling you what he wants."

The coffee arrived, and before they could start to drink it, Brandon's father arrived. He barged into the office as if he owned the place. He was a big man with a florid face and arrogant blue eyes. "Are you Santiago?"

"Yes, are you Mr. Reynolds?" Santiago said, extending his hand politely.

"I want an explanation," Reynolds said, ignoring the invitation for a handshake.

"We'll be happy to give you one. Would you like some coffee?"

"No, thanks. I don't have time for coffee."

"Then please sit down. This is Sister Maura, the head of our disciplinary committee."

"I'm glad to meet you," Maura said truthfully.

Still standing, Reynolds told them: "I'm an attorney, and I'm prepared to take legal action against you."

"Okay," Santiago said respectfully. "Would you like to present your arguments?"

"According to my son, you have no evidence against him."

"We have a lot of evidence against him," Maura said. "To begin with, the victim identified him out of a lineup."

"How could she have identified him? She never saw the faces of the guys."

"How do you know she never saw their faces?"

"My son told me, and I believe him."

"If he wasn't at the scene of the crime, how would he know she never saw their faces?"

"Someone made a video of it."

"And your son watched the video?"

"I know he shouldn't have, but there're so many bad things on the internet for the kids to watch, including those beheadings. Anyway, he said that in the video the girl was blindfolded, so she couldn't have seen their faces."

"Well, she didn't identify him from his face," Maura said. "She identified him from his voice. We had her listen to eight guys, who all read the same passage to her, and with no hesitation she identified the three guys who raped her."

"She could have guessed them," Reynolds said.

"She had one chance in fifty-six of guessing all three of them correctly."

"Is that all you have?" Reynolds asked after a silence.

"No, we have more. One of the guys who participated in the rape identified your son."

"He lied, and he has a reason to lie. He's jealous of my son. He didn't make the lacrosse team, and Brandon did."

Now seeing a use for the information the police captain had given her, Maura said: "We have more evidence. The guys who raped her were drinking beer on the site where it happened. They left behind more than a dozen crumpled beer cans. And your son's fingerprints were on four of the cans."

For the first time Reynolds looked worried. "How do you know they were my son's prints?"

"The Yonkers police matched them with the prints of a Brandon Reynolds, who was arrested last year and charged with raping a high school girl."

"That charge was dismissed, and anyway it has no relevance."

"It has relevance for identifying your son as one of the guys who was at the site where this girl was raped."

"He could have been there at a different time."

"He could have, but it's adding up."

Reynolds paced and finally stopped. "So maybe he was there at the time when the girl claims she was raped. But he says she consented to it. And if she consented, then it wasn't rape."

"Have you seen the video?" Santiago asked.

"No, I haven't. I don't watch that kind of stuff."

"Well, you should see it." Santiago got up and brought his laptop from his desk and set it on the conference table. He took a flash drive out of his pocket and plugged it in. "Your son plays a starring role it."

The three of them sat at the conference table with Reynolds in the middle.

It was the third time Maura had seen at least parts of the video, and each time it got worse. Only this time she noticed something that had escaped her before.

After playing the last scene, in which the guy urinated on the girl, Santiago asked: "Do you honestly believe that any girl would consent to that indignity?"

"I don't know," Reynolds said lamely. "Kids do kinky things."

"Please play that scene again," Maura said.

Santiago played the scene again.

"Now, stop right there. Do you see the right arm of the guy who's urinating on her?"

"Yeah, I see it," Reynolds admitted.

"What do you see on the guy's forearm?"

"I see a tattoo of lacrosse sticks."

"And what does your son have on his right forearm?"

"A tattoo of lacrosse sticks," Reynolds said almost in a whisper.

"I know it's hard," Santiago said, "to believe your son would do such a thing. But after seeing that video you have to believe it. And instead of enabling him to continue doing such things, you have to call him to account. If you don't, then the next time he'll do something worse, and you'll be responsible."

For a while Reynolds was silent, gazing at the blank screen of the laptop, and then with both hands he covered his eyes and sobbed: "Oh, God. What did I do wrong?"

Santiago asked her to stay after Reynolds had left, implying that he had something to tell her, so she sat down across from him, prepared to listen.

He began by saying: "I talked with our lawyer about making them take that video off the internet, and he agreed that we could do it. But while we talked, I asked him if we could charge them with using our campus to promote violence against women."

Maura waited for him to continue.

"He said we could, and with all the evidence we have, he thinks we have a very good chance of winning the case."

"What would that mean?"

"It would mean that if those guys were convicted, they could get three to five years in prison. Which is the least that they deserve," Santiago added.

"Would Esperanza have to testify?"

"He says she wouldn't. She wouldn't be the plaintiff. We'd be the plaintiff."

"What about Jeffrey?"

"He'd have to testify, but through plea bargaining he'd probably get off with a year of community service."

"That sounds fair."

"So what do you think?"

"I think it would serve the cause of justice," Maura said, "and as long as Esperanza doesn't get dragged into it, I think you should do it."

Santiago smiled faintly. "I noticed that you said 'you' not 'we' should do it."

"My role isn't to pursue justice. That's your role. My role is to pursue mercy, and that's enough for one imperfect human being."

"Okay, sister. I accept that division of labor."

Back in her office, Maura only had time to help a student with her course schedule for the spring semester when Wendy appeared, asking "Do you have a minute?"

"Yeah, come in."

After sitting down Wendy asked: "Did your committee make a decision?"

"It did, and since you helped us, I can tell you what it is. But it's confidential information."

"I understand. I won't tell anyone."

"We decided that Esperanza was raped."

"That should have been a no brainer, but I know what happens in these cases."

"We also decided to expel the three guys who raped her and only to suspend the guy who pinned her arms."

"Will anything else happen to them?"

"The college is going to charge them with using our campus to promote violence against women, and if they're convicted, they could get three to five years in prison."

"Now, that's beginning to sound like justice."

"So are you satisfied?"

"Yeah. But I've been thinking about my mission. I mean, after what you told me in our last meeting. And I decided that my mission should be to help the victims of violence against women, not to punish the perpetrators. So I'm changing my major from criminal justice to counseling."

"I'm glad you made that decision."

"Thanks. I already know about Esperanza, so maybe I could start with her."

"You could join our team."

"You'd accept me?"

"Of course. We need a student with your experience."

"Maybe we could have a support group at the college for girls who've been harassed by guys. There are so many ways we can be harassed, short of being raped."

"That's a great idea," Maura said. "We have a faculty member who would be ideal as a mentor for that kind of group."

"I want to thank you for opening my eyes," Wendy said after a pause. "I mean, to the fact that not all guys are like the ones who raped me."

"I want to thank you for reconsidering your position, for giving me a good teaching experience."

Wendy rose from the chair, saying: "Well, I have to take a plane to Ohio this afternoon."

"Are you going home for Thanksgiving?"

"Yeah. I missed the last one, but now I think I can handle it."

"Have a happy Thanksgiving."

"You too, sister."

Maura sat at her desk, knowing that today and tomorrow the resident students would be going home for Thanksgiving. Some had already left, and by tomorrow afternoon the campus would be empty, except for the flock of Canadian geese who no longer remembered how to fly south for the winter. On Thanksgiving the convent served a lunch of turkey with all the trimmings, but only a few nuns who had no remaining families attended, so there were always leftovers for the soup kitchen at San Pedro. In fact, the leftovers were sent down there in time for dinner.

As usual Maura would have lunch in the convent to keep the surviving nuns company, but she didn't relish the thought of spending the evening alone in her room. Audrey was gone now seven years, and Solana would be with her family in the Bronx. She could think of only one person who might be available, and she sent him a text message, suggesting they meet at Hogan's.

From the times she had gone there with Audrey she knew that Hogan's would be open on Thanksgiving. Few bars or restaurants were open then, enabling their employees to spend the holiday with their families, but with so many patrons who for various reasons didn't have families, the owners of Hogan's felt it was their duty to be open for Thanksgiving, and from noon on they had a carving board with roast turkey breast, accompanied by steam trays of mashed potatoes, stuffing, green beans, and carrots, plus gravy and cranberry sauce. It was the next best thing to the food at a Blarney Stone in the city.

When she arrived there at five thirty on Thanksgiving the place was filled with the usual guys and a few women, most of them talking at the same time. Paul was in a booth with a glass of Guinness in front of him. He got up and gave her a holiday hug, and then he ordered a Dewar's on the rocks for her, knowing what she wanted.

"I hear you have a guest at the rectory," she said after sipping her drink.

"I do," Paul said. "He went home on Wednesday, but he'll be back on Sunday evening."

"I assume he'll help you with odd jobs."

"Oh, yeah. And he knows how to cook, so I'll have better meals."

She surveyed his face. It was lined from smoking, but he still looked young and full of hope. It occurred to her, not for the first time, that he could be her son.

"Jeffrey told me what your committee decided, so you don't have to bring me up to date on that. But what about Esperanza? How's she doing?"

"She's doing okay, considering what happened to her."

"Do you think there's any chance for a reconciliation between her and Jeffrey?"

"I think there is, but it's going to take time."

"Well, he started working at the food pantry, and I'll keep finding good things for him to do. So maybe it'll happen."

Looking around her, Maura said: "They don't have this holiday in Ireland."

"No, they don't. I guess it's not in the Irish temperament to be thankful."

She understood. "Yeah, I guess it's not. My grandmother never understood why we have Thanksgiving. But she always put a lot of food on the table."

"They have a lot of food on the table here. Have you eaten?"

"Not really. I had lunch in the convent with the nuns who have nowhere else to go, but I only picked at my plate. I was depressed by the thought that in a few more years I'll be just like them, with nowhere else to go."

"You'll always have Hogan's."

"Yeah, but will I always have you?"

"I'm not due to be reassigned for another five years, and maybe by then they won't have anyone to replace me, so they'll keep me here."

"Is there any chance they'll close your parish?"

"No chance at all. We were nowhere near being on the recent list of mergers or closures. We have a lot of young families, who are having children."

"That's good. I hope to see them as students at the college."

"Come on," he said. "Let's get some food."

She followed him to the carving board, suddenly hungry, and she returned to the booth with a full plate of turkey with all the trimmings.

When Paul had given thanks for the food, Maura added: "And thank you, Lord, for helping Jeffrey and Esperanza to start the process of reconciliation."

"Amen," he said, reaching for his glass of Guinness.

BOOK CLUB GUIDE TO

The Silver Locket

Tom Milton

Introduction

Esperanza Vargas is happily walking along a path that overlooks the Hudson River, feeling safe because she's on a college campus, when suddenly from behind her a strong arm locks around her neck and chokes her unconscious. The next thing she knows, she's being raped by four guys, who have blindfolded her, gagged her, and stripped her naked. When all except one of them have taken their turn, they leave her to deal with what they have done to her. Removing the blindfold, she finds herself in a wooded area hidden from the path, and the sun has gone down. Instinctively, she reaches for the silver locket that her parents gave her for her fifteenth birthday, which she wears on a chain around her neck, but it's no longer there. She crawls around in the darkness desperately looking for it, but she doesn't find it.

She lives with her parents about three miles from the college but she can't go home in her present condition, so she contacts a friend who lives in the dormitory. Her friend, whose name is Griselda, responds to her plight and invites her into the dormitory where she can shower and wash her clothes. She doesn't tell the friend what happened to her, and she doesn't tell her parents after she gets home. She lies about why she got home late, and she hopes that her parents will never learn what happened to her, especially because she's afraid that her father will believe it was somehow her fault.

In the meantime, Jeffrey, the guy who pinned her arms while the other three guys raped her but didn't take his turn, is racked with guilt for what he did. The next morning, he returns to the scene of the crime, where he finds a silver locket that must have been ripped from a chain around the girl's neck. He opens the locket and inside he sees a picture of the Blessed Mother, who he later identifies as Our Lady of Guadalupe. Imagining how the girl must feel to have lost the locket, he intends to return it to her. He gets support in this intention from a local priest, and when he sees the girl on campus two days later he tries to return the locket to her. But she won't take it, leaving him stuck with this reminder of what he did to her.

A teacher, Sister Maura, who has Esperanza and Jeffrey in separate classes, can tell from their behavior that something is wrong, and she notices that Esperanza's locket is missing, but the girl won't tell her anything. The boy tells Sister Maura that he did something unforgivable, but he won't tell her what it was. Then finally he comes to her office and asks her to return the locket to Esperanza, revealing that whatever he did that was unforgivable, he did to Esperanza. Hoping that the locket will give him an opportunity to talk with the girl, Sister Maura tells him he should return it himself, and he agrees to try again.

Esperanza has begun to worry that she might get pregnant, and she learns from Griselda, who has a worldly older sister, about morning-after pills and pregnancy tests. She knows that if she gets pregnant she won't be about to conceal what happened, and she is terrified by the prospect. When her mother notices that the locket is missing, she lies about what happened to it, and gradually her life becomes a series of lies. To make matters worse, a girl stops her on campus and tells her that the guys made a video of what they did to her, and that they have posted it on a website. The girl, whose name is Wendy, shows her a picture from the video that clearly reveals her identity. She learns that Wendy had a similar experience at another college, and that she transferred to this college in the hope of starting her life over, but she has a mission to bring to justice guys who commit violence against women on college campuses. Esperanza wants nothing to do with this mission, she only wants to conceal what happened, but now that a video of her being raped has been posted on a website, she realizes that sooner or later what happened to her will become public knowledge. So she starts the process of telling the truth by telling Griselda what happened to her. Griselda urges her to tell her parents, which she still can't bring herself to do.

After trying again to return the locket to Esperanza without success, Jeffrey goes to Sister Maura and again asks her to return the locket. She tells him she knows what he did to Esperanza, and he finally opens up and tells her everything, including the fact that a video of the rape has been posted on a website. A few days later, Wendy brings her a copy of the video, knowing that Sister Maura is head of the disciplinary committee, and wanting to provide evidence that can be used to prosecute the guys who raped Esperanza. The problem is, unless Esperanza brings her case to the disciplinary committee, they can't pursue it.

Though her father isn't the type of man who would watch videos of gang rapes, he is shown the video by a former employee whom he fired, and he is enraged. Though Esperanza insists that what he saw in the video wasn't her fault, her father will only believe she was innocent if she presses charges against the guys and wins her case. So, reluctantly, she begins the process by telling Sister Maura she will bring her case to the disciplinary committee. She's hoping that a unanimous decision by the committee in her favor will be enough to satisfy her father.

A conversation with Tom Milton

In this novel you address the issue of violence against women, which occurs everywhere—in the home, in schools, on college campuses, on the streets, in the workplace, and in war zones. Why did you set this novel on a college campus?

Violence against women has become a major issue on college campuses, with surveys indicating that a large number of women on campus have been victims of sexual harassment and rape. We want to believe that college campuses, like homes, or schools, or churches, are places where our children are safe from violence. We know they're not safe on the streets or in war zones, but we want to believe they're safe on college campuses, just as the victim in this novel believes she's safe on the campus of St. Catherine College. The reality is, as long as we have a culture that tolerates and even promotes violence, our children aren't safe anywhere.

In addressing this issue you created three characters, with three different points of view on what happened. One point of view is that of the victim, Esperanza. Another point of view is that of a perpetrator, Jeffrey. And the third point of view is that of Sister Maura, who wants to bring about a reconciliation between them. What was your purpose in telling this story from three points of view?

My purpose was not only to address the issue of violence against women, but also to explore its effects on victims, perpetrators, and people who want to do something about it, which includes people who want to stop it as well as people who want to mitigate its consequences. By presenting the victim's point of view, I can show how she was affected by it. Of course I realize that victims of rape are individuals who have different feelings about the experience, but they also must have some feelings in common with the victim in this story.

I think one of those feelings in common is that even though this victim is in no way responsible for what happened to her—she wasn't wearing provocative clothes, she wasn't drinking, she wasn't at a party—she still has the feeling that somehow it was her fault, and that her father in particular will blame her for what happened.

I could tell you horror stories about fathers who blame their daughters for being sexually abused. They assume that somehow their daughters asked for it. That's why I wanted a victim who was completely innocent, who was pure and religious, who wore a silver locket on a chain around her neck with a picture of Our Lady of Guadalupe inside. There was no way she asked for it.

Are you suggesting that her father's reaction is typical?

It may not be typical, but from what I've heard from victims it's far too common. Now, at some deep level, this reaction might arise from the father's feeling that somehow he failed to protect his daughter, and instead of blaming himself, he blames her.

That's understandable. There also might be a feeling on the part of the victim that she failed to protect something of value to her father.

And having failed to protect it, she's under great pressure to prove her innocence.

That brings up another feeling in common. She wants to prove her innocence, but she doesn't want to go through the process of charging her attackers and going to court.

She knows that a very small percentage of such cases lead to convictions, and meanwhile she would be exposing her family to shame.

You mean she's afraid that the public will believe that somehow it was her fault.

Yes. So in addition to the personal guilt she feels, she'll also have to deal with public shame.

I want to come back to Esperanza, but let's talk about Jeffrey for a moment. You've presented us with a good kid, who's sensitive and responsible and also religious. How do you expect us to believe that he would participate in a gang rape?

As one of my other characters says, guys in gangs are capable of doing anything. Alone, he never would have done such a thing. With one other guy, he wouldn't have done it. But in a gang of four guys, with the peer pressure to go along with them, Jeffrey is capable of doing anything.

He pins her arms while the other guys rape her. He doesn't take his turn with her, but later he compares himself with the guy who pinned the arms of Christ while they were nailing him to the cross. I think your image says everything about how he feels. But why should we care about his feelings after what he did to Esperanza?

We should care about his feelings because there's hope for him. As you know, the first steps in the process of reconciliation are to acknowledge the evil we have done, to feel remorse, and to want forgiveness. We see Jeffrey going through these steps.

It took me a while to realize that the main theme of this novel is reconciliation. And I know you deliberately presented us with a situation where it's almost impossible for us to imagine a reconciliation.

It's almost impossible, but not impossible.

Well, let's talk about the third point of view, the nun who knows both of these young people, learns what happened, and wants to help them find a way to reconciliation. We've seen Sister Maura before in three of your novels—All the Flowers, Outside the Gate, *and* Orphans of War—*playing minor but important roles. But now we see her in a major role. Is she your alter ego?*

I wouldn't go that far, but she definitely does what I would like to see myself doing in the situations where she appears.

You make it clear that in this situation her goal is mercy, not justice.

Mercy is what these two young people need. She leaves justice to the president of the college, who will pursue it for his own reasons.

You know, when the leader posted a video of the rape on a website, I thought you were exaggerating. So I checked, and I was appalled to discover that there are dozens of websites that have videos of gang rapes. Who would watch such videos?

The same people who watch videos of terrorists cutting off the heads of their captives. They watch those videos to satisfy a lust for violence.

Do you think watching videos of gang rapes promotes gang rapes?

Of course it does. It conditions the viewers to regard women as appropriate objects of violence.

I notice that you didn't say objects of sex.

It has nothing to do with sex. It has everything to do with violence. And being cowards, they target women because on average women are physically smaller and weaker than men—like Esperanza, who weighs ninety pounds.

Against four guys with an average weight of one hundred and eighty-five pounds.

So obviously she was an innocent victim. But ultimately this novel is about the possibility of a reconciliation between her and Jeffrey, and while I have doubts about that happening, I do believe there's hope for them.

Discussion questions

1. Why does Esperanza feel that her being raped was somehow her fault?

2. Why does she expect her father to blame her?

3. Does she do enough to get support from her mother?

4. Should she have pursued justice against the guys who raped her?

5. Why does she refuse to accept the locket when Jeffrey tries to return it to her?

6. Why did Jeffrey, a well-raised young man, participate in a gang rape?

7. Should Jeffrey have done more to stop Brandon from posting the video on a website?

8. Was it helpful for Jeffrey to intercede with Esperanza's father?

9. How does the locket function as a propellant of action in this novel?

10. What thematic meaning do you attribute to the locket?

11. What is Sister Maura's goal? To what extent do you think she achieved it?

12. What role does Father Paul play in the story? How important for the story is his relationship with Sister Maura?

13. What role does Sister Solana play in the story? Do you think her attempts to help Esperanza make a difference?

14. What role does Griselda play? What do you think is the pivotal point of her relationship with Esperanza?

15. What role does Wendy play? How is she influenced by Sister Maura?

16. How important is the setting of this story?

17. Why did the author use three points of view to tell this story?

18. Do you think there will be a reconciliation between Esperanza and Jeffrey?

CPSIA information can be obtained at www.ICGtesting.com
Printed in the USA
LVOW07s0438191016

509291LV00011BA/17/P